MORNING WAS NEVER JOHN COFFIN'S BEST TIME

He was shaving while drinking a mug of coffee. Damn the bell! Ignore it. No, impossible to ignore it. On and on ringing.

A minute later, and Coffin was running down the street, shaving and coffee unfinished.

Into No. 22, the front door left open wide by Mrs. Brocklebank in her flight, then to the dining room.

"My God."

They were all three at the table where they had been sitting at a meal, the curry soup before them, a dreadful static group, posed for a stage set.

Edward had fallen forward, Irene had sagged toward the floor and Nona still sat there, upright, supported by the arm of the chair.

But dead. They were all dead.

⎯⎯⎯⎯⎯⎯ ★ ⎯⎯⎯⎯⎯⎯

COFFIN UNDERGROUND

Gwendoline Butler

TORONTO • NEW YORK • LONDON
AMSTERDAM • PARIS • SYDNEY • HAMBURG
STOCKHOLM • ATHENS • TOKYO • MILAN
MADRID • WARSAW • BUDAPEST • AUCKLAND

*I have to acknowledge the help of John Kennedy
Melling in providing me with material and
information about fantasy games and their
influence.*

COFFIN UNDERGROUND

A Worldwide Mystery/December 1992

First published by St Martin's Press Incorporated.

ISBN 0-373-26110-1

9 drops of human blood
7 grains of gunpowder
½ ounce of putrefied brain
13 mashed graveworms

*Recipe for Horror provided
by
Mary and Percy Bysshe Shelley*

PROLOGUE

ONE HOT DAY in the summer of 1974, in New York, a young girl was out shopping. She was looking for a present for her boyfriend back in England. It would soon be his birthday, he was three years older than she was, and when they had parted she had made a promise that she would send him a present. In many ways she felt very far away from him now and getting farther with every minute, but she meant to keep that promise. She had not written many letters to him, although he had sent her constant messages of a brief if loving kind. The fact was that her world and his were now so very different. Her parents were working in New York, her father in the United Nations and her mother for a private consultancy, and they were living in a smart secure part of the city. She was a diplomat's child and used to that way of life; her London boyfriend was in different circumstances altogether.

She had some errands to do for her mother in a big and famous store in Fifth Avenue (her mother shopped expensively), so that her first search for a present was in this store. This kind of shop was her natural habitat since her family had both taste and money. But today nothing took her fancy as a suitable present.

There was a reason for this, one of which she might not have been fully aware herself. She was in an odd mood, had been for some weeks now. Puberty was hitting her hard. Sex was both interesting her and perturbing her. She did not quite know how to handle it or herself. She was changing so fast that every day she felt different. It puzzled her as much as anyone.

Her parents sensed something of her emotional disturbance, but put it down to her arrival at an awkward age, in a new and exciting city. She was a clever girl, doing well at her private school. In this way New York suited her. Ambition was stirring inside her.

She strolled around the store, studying ties, shirts, small leather goods and pieces of jewellery, like gold chains such as men wear. He would like such a chain, but although well provided with money for her age, she was still a child who could not afford gold.

She wandered into the book department. No, nothing he would like there. He was not a reader. More an adventurer in life, or that was how he saw himself. But looking at the books had given her an idea. She remembered something that one of her mother's friends in London, a distinguished man, had told her about. And hadn't her friends at school here joked about some similar game? She poked about for what she fancied.

She could feel her heart beginning to bang. It was exciting, her idea. But no, she soon realized that this was not the sort of store in which to find what she wanted. Too staid, too conventional.

In fact, she fancied the sales assistant gave her an odd look when she asked by name for what she wanted, but this might have been her imagination. It was saleable, after all. No, they did not stock it. Well, she was not surprised.

She was a robust girl who had been through all the upheavals attendant upon the life of a diplomat's family with vivacity and pleasure. She liked the excitement. They had a house in London, England, to which they returned at intervals. It was not a house she enjoyed living in, although she liked London. The house had a feeling about it which she noticed on her first entrance every time the family returned. After that first impact, she got used to it. Or it faded away. She would call it a house with a strong character and not all of it nice. It was a house with a history.

She might write about it in a story for her class magazine. She wanted to get one in this term if she could. It would be good for her standing amongst her peers. But there was another episode in her London life she might write about. Get it out on paper and stop thinking about it, she decided.

In the next shop, she bought a fresh pad of paper to use for her writing. Then she made her inquiry.

Oh yes, they had the game. Yes, certainly, it could be packed up ready to send overseas. The assistant was surprised. This was not the type of kid that usually bought these games. Typically, they were white, well educated and pushy. This girl was well spoken but fulfilled no other condition.

The girl adopted a sophisticated air and made all the arrangements for postage and the US Customs. The assistant had given her a look of surprise, as if she wasn't the sort of person who usually bought that kind of game, but so what?

The palms of her hands were sweating as she completed the transaction. Her imagination was excited. Various tales were going the rounds about this game in her circle. The phrase 'Playing with Fire' came into her mind.

ONE

THE HOUSE STOOD by the church and by the church was the churchyard which the house had done its share to fill. More than its share, in truth.

There was already another body about to take up residence but no one knew about that yet.

The past, of course, was different.

In the last century, when the house in Greenwich was only a few years old, a visitor from abroad had brought cholera with him from India, which had spread through the district after killing him. A lot of new graves appeared in St Luke's churchyard at this time.

Nor had the house, No. 22, Church Row, ceased in its work of filling graves. In addition to what you might call the average statistical supply of family bodies, inhabitants of the house, dying in the usual way from old age, childbirth or the poor medicine of the period, the house picked up other victims. It attracted the blast from a bomb dropped by a Zeppelin in World War One and from a landmine in the second great war. Neither was a direct hit, but each time there were many casualties in the house, which seemed to fill up for the occasion of a calamity as if it knew one was coming and wanted to do its best. Or worst. In 1917 when the Zeppelin hung over Greenwich the house was crowded with a party of young soldiers, home from the trenches and celebrating the twenty-first birthday of the son of the house. As it turned out he would have been safer in the trenches. (His twin sister survived the blast but the house got her in the end, because she died, with her parents and younger sister, in the great influenza epidemic of 1918.) In 1941 the house was used as a hostel for nurses working in the nearby Dreadnought Seaman's Hospital, the owner being abroad on war service and his wife and family evacuated. Most of the nurses were killed, and of those that died, some, being local girls, were interred in one great grave in St Luke's.

A quiet time set in for No. 22, Church Row after the war. It had had enough. Or it was resting.

In 1972 the then owner of the house, a career diplomat, was abroad with his family (he came back the next year, and then in 1975 left for New York), and the house was let to three students in the University of London who were enrolled in Goldsmiths' College at New Cross. They were quiet, unobtrusive lads, not much seen and no trouble to anyone.

Since the other inhabitants of the street did not see them regularly, they were not at first much missed. No one saw them come in, no one saw them go.

But they did go somewhere because they were never seen alive again, leaving a lot of blood behind in the house. Blood on the stairs and in the kitchen on the ground floor. So it was told.

In 1978 a policeman called John Coffin, now a Chief Superintendent, moved into Church Row, and heard all the stories about the house and treated the superstition with the contempt it deserved.

He was able to do so, of course, since he was not living at No. 22 (although he knew the present owners) but at No. 5, well away from any dangerous emanations.

It was Mrs Brocklebank, who cleaned his house and also did for No. 22, who told him the saga. She could even add to the story, and did, the moment she saw her chance.

'Oh, come on now, Mrs B. It's all rubbish. Houses can't do that sort of thing. You mustn't be superstitious. And as for the students, was there really any blood? I heard they just moonlighted, left without paying their rent.'

'Never been seen again, though, have they?'

'Well, I don't know about that.' He did not know the details of the case, if indeed there had been one. He seemed to remember there was some puzzle about the three students. Ot was it just one of them?

But for Mrs Brocklebank the blood was an indelible part of the story. Literally so.

'Every time I clean that house on the anniversary of the disappearance there is blood on the front step. I have to scrub it away.'

'Oh, Mrs B.'

'Never really get it off. It's always there. Faintly. But worse on that day.'

'Did you see the blood in the house yourself, then?'

'Well, no. Wasn't working for Mrs Pitt then, was I? In the soap factory, Deller's, I was, before I decided to better myself. But we all heard. Everyone knew about it.'

She admired her new employer. You'd never know he was a policeman, she told herself.

He was a tall man, thinner than he had been, thinner perhaps than nature intended, a long face with fair hair just beginning to show traces of grey. He had never been good-looking but experience, life itself, had drawn on his face the lines which gave him distinction. His eyes still had the hopeful look which had been his as a boy. If you did not have hope in the world of London streets in which he had grown up, you had nothing, and never would have. It was this look which had drawn Mrs Brocklebank to tell him about the blood. Tell him, she'd advised herself. Get it off your chest.

Coffin deliberately went to take a look at the step of No. 22 one day, and it was true there was a string of faint stains that could have been blood on the two shallow stone steps to the front door. But they could have been a lot of other things as well.

No. 22 was a quiet dark house of three storeys, possibly a shade gloomy but otherwise unremarkable, and identical to the house where he had recently moved into the top flat.

Nothing in it, all rubbish, he thought. Just a house that has got a bad name. And he thought of all the other such houses there were. Blythswood Square; Rillington Place; The Priory, Balham.

But he was interested enough to make some inquiries about the case of the missing students.

His opportunity came when he had to deal with a local sergeant about another case. A violent criminal, William Howard Egan, had just come out of prison after serving his term and was known to be looking for revenge on the informer who had helped to put him there. The fact that this informer was his son-in-law, Terence Place, was not going to stop him. Both hunter and hunted were believed to be hiding in South London, and they might be in Greenwich. John Coffin had been the detective on the case. Threats had been made against him too by Egan. He was taking a personal interest.

'I don't think Billy Egan's here, but that isn't to say he won't be, or isn't, he was always a cunning bastard. He has a taste for this part of the world, so he might be back. I'll keep my eyes open. You can count on me.'

'Thanks, Bernard.' Coffin took his chance. 'What's this tale I hear about three students going missing from a house in Church Row? Anything in it?' He remembered a bit himself, but not the details.

The sergeant was an older man, passed over for promotion, but content to be what he was, and a great well of information about the district, which he transmitted only when it suited him, it was his property. He had lived in this part of South London all his life. Bernard Jones had known John Coffin when he was a humble detective, well before he had shot up the ladder so successfully. He was far too tactful to dwell on this, or even to mention it. It coloured their relationship, though, loading it with memories of old cases, old criminals and older colleagues.

The two men were having a sandwich and a cup of tea in the police canteen in Royal Hill police station where Jones was based. He didn't want to talk about students, missing or not, he wanted a gossip.

About crime in his patch.

'Been fairly quiet here lately. Two bodies found roped together in the river. Black man, white woman. The forensics say it could be suicide. Old man found dead in the street. Been dead over a week when found on a main road. Can you beat it? I suppose they thought he was put out for the dustmen. Two dead babies in a suitcase. No, nothing special.'

Or gossip about old friends.

'So Dander slipped off the side.'

'Yes.' Coffin looked serious. Commander Dander had been his patron and friend. 'And I didn't even known he was ill till he went. Very sudden. Heart. Still, it wasn't a bad way to go.'

'What he would have wanted.'

'Don't know about that.' Coffin remembered his Dander. 'If he'd had what he wanted, I think he would have lived for ever.'

'Hard on his wife, though.'

'Which? Dying suddenly or living for ever?'

'With Charley Dander I should think living for ever would be the worst punishment.'

'Did you know he had three wives?' said Coffin. 'We none of us knew till they all turned up at the funeral. All divorced and all hating the sight of each other.'

'I bet they were lookers. Dander knew how to pick them.'

And leave them, thought Coffin, a man loyal to his mates but not to his women.

'I hear you're living in Church Row?'

Coffin nodded.

'Nice houses, but a bit near the churchyard for my taste.' So the sergeant, who knew everything, had heard the tales about the powers of No. 22.

'I'm the other end.'

'Just as well.'

'So I've heard.'

The sergeant laughed.

Coffin tried once more: 'What's this tale about three students disappearing from a house in the Row, leaving a lot of blood behind and never being seen again?'

The sergeant sighed. 'That old tale going round again? They didn't disappear. Or not for long. There was a bit of blood about, though. What happened was, the three of them had a fight, got a lot of blood on the furnishings and lost their nerve about the damage they'd done. I think they did drop out of sight for a few days, but not more. The College soon got on to them.'

'I'm beginning to remember some of the details myself now. It's coming back. There was something later about one of the students, though, wasn't there?'

Bernard Jones picked up his sandwich, inspecting it. 'They put less and less ham in these every day, I say. But they say they don't. More if anything. One day I'll measure.'

'Yes, that's the scientific approach.'

The sergeant ate the sandwich in three great mouthfuls, talking between bites. 'Something about one of the students, Malcolm Kincaid. He was a chemistry student. A year after he graduated, he was found dead in Greenwich Park. His body was lying tucked away in some bushes. Killed himself. Left a note saying he was going to do it. He did it with cyanide, he'd managed to lift a quantity from the lab where he was working. It's a quick death. The medical evidence was that he died almost instantaneously.'

'So what?' It was obvious there was something.

'Nothing to show how he'd taken it, no container, no poison, although he'd stolen a good few grams. In the form of potassium cyanide which would have gone down better if dissolved in liquid. Caused a lot of worry, that did.'

'But he had left a note saying he was going to kill himself?'

'Oh yes, it was there with him. And he had the motive. That came out: girl trouble and money worries. He was a bit of a depressive too. Yes, he meant to do it.'

'So what was the worry?'

'Looking as though someone else had been there. He was all neat and tidied up. When you take cyanide you don't die that way.'

Coffin thought about it. 'Interesting. What happened then?'

Bernard shrugged. 'A verdict of suicide was reluctantly arrived at.'

'When was this?'

Bernard worked it out. 'About three years ago. Just over.'

'One of life's little mysteries,' said Coffin.

Then the talk turned to other things, and he buried the story of Malcolm Kincaid, student, at the back of his mind.

One of those puzzles you think about in the middle of the night and can never decide on an answer. It could go in the drawer with Mr Qualtrough of Menlove Gardens East, and where was the axe that killed the Bordens?

He thought a bit about William Egan the grudge-bearer, and kept on his guard, but there was no sign of him. Nor any movement in the undergrowth of the local criminal jungle that might show his passage. Once or twice he thought he saw Mrs Brocklebank, that conveyer of news around the town, giving him a thoughtful look as if she knew something he did not, but that probably meant nothing more than that she was news-gathering.

He liked the new flat in Church Row, where over the roofs and through the trees he could see the top of the clipper, the *Cutty Sark*. At the moment the trees blocked his view, but in winter when the leaves had thinned he would be able to see the intricate rigging of the ship. He liked that thought. Living here was bringing him back to an area he had known as a boy and where he had worked at the beginning of his career. It was a part of London for which he retained an affection. For ten years he had been living away from the suburb, he had moved off deliberately, there were mixed memories, some good and just a few downright painful, but now he was glad to be back. It felt like home. It was amazing how life stitched itself together again into a piece if you gave it a chance.

Every time he walked down Church Row on the way to work, he took a look at No. 22. It had been empty for some months since the last tenants had left. Then one day he saw the windows had been washed and plants put in the window-boxes. In the spring, they were daffodils. Yes, said Mrs B, the owner and his family are coming back. Edward Pitt had retired from the FO; he had been working at the United Nations. John Coffin was looking forward to meeting him again, a friendly, vital man, as he recalled. The whole family was interesting. People said they were artistic and amusing. They had a few critics too, but that was understandable. There had been 'family' problems, whatever that meant, but even the easiest of families did not always see eye to eye. Interesting to watch how they got on in No. 22, where by all accounts they had never lived much. He might find out what they knew of the story of the three students. He looked down at the front steps. No real sign of blood.

Blood.

He had got his life settled: he had got someone reliable to clean his place in Mrs Brocklebank, who, he now realized, 'did' for most of the road, and who had really acquired him rather than the other way round; and he had arranged for two newspapers to be delivered daily, and had settled on a milkman who also sold milk and eggs. You could live on bread, milk and eggs if you had to. Everything was in train. The only drawback was that Mrs Brocklebank would not iron his shirts. Or anything of his.

'I do Brock's and that's my lot.' It was the first time he had realized there was a living Mr Brocklebank; he had supposed her to be a widow. She had the vigorous healthy look of a woman who lived for herself alone.

He tried drip-drying his shirts himself, but he liked the cuffs ironed. He tried ironing them himself. It was easy if you didn't scorch them. He did scorch them. Quite often. Too often.

He sought help.

Mrs Brocklebank surveyed the burnt offerings without sympathy. 'It's quite simple if you keep the heat on the iron adjusted.'

'I do keep it adjusted. But it leaps up.'

'I'm not a laundress myself.' She considered; Coffin waited hopefully. 'I suppose you could try Sarah Fleming. Sal has a good hand with the iron, she ought to have with the practice she gets looking after that brood of hers, and she's usually glad to earn an extra pound or two.'

He left the arrangements to her, with the result that she took away his washing on a Monday and it reappeared, neatly packaged and with the bill, on his doormat every Wednesday. Mrs Brocklebank acted as banker.

Occasionally messages came back through Mrs B.

'Sal says you need a new blue shirt. The cuffs are frayed and it's not worth the trouble of ironing.'

Sal obviously had high standards. He bought a couple of new blue shirts.

'Sal says could you try not to get lipstick on your collar.' This message was delivered with a light smirk. 'She says it's hard to get off.'

'It's red ink,' said Coffin, lying.

Living as a bachelor, and at the moment wifeless, he was not celibate. But he felt it was his business and not Sarah Fleming's. Sal, he decided, could look after her own affairs, if she had any apart from laundry, and leave his alone. Old witch.

Two weeks had passed. There was no news of either William Egan or his son-in-law but the daughter had taken herself off to Spain. It might mean something, or it might mean no more than that she had had enough of both father and husband. The general feeling was that she had a right to such a reaction.

But the Pitts had arrived home and No. 22 was looking lively. Windows opened to let the sun in, new curtains and a big car parked outside the door. John Coffin had not met them again yet, but had seen them once or twice as he passed and given a wave. Whether he was remembered or not he was unsure, but diplomacy and good manners prevailed, so that he got a wave back. Edward Pitt was tall and handsome, every bit the diplomat. With white hair he looked older than he probably was, just as his wife looked younger. Irene Pitt was still youthful, a pretty curly-haired woman with bright eyes and skin with a shine on it. But the beauty of the family was the daughter, a slender, leggy creature of fifteen years. She had joined a smart London girls' school and disappeared on the train every day to her studies. There was a younger boy who had been recruited to the local public school, and heaven help him there, said Mrs Brocklebank. She added the information that Mr Pitt, although retired from the Foreign Service, was going to join the foreign bureau of a London newspaper, and that Mrs Pitt, who was an economist, intended to find some work too. She was a lot younger than her husband. There were also a dog and a cat to join the household but they were at present in quarantine.

That concluded her head count, but she added the news that the Pitts would be giving a party for friends and neighbours to celebrate their return.

Nothing was said about the bad character of the house, but Coffin felt it hung there like a grim smile on the face of a friend.

No sign anywhere of William Egan, but his son-in-law had been spotted once down by the river. He had got on a bus and disappeared in the direction of Woolwich before he could be stopped.

The contact who claimed to have seen him, a GBH man of many violent episodes and many incarcerations, now going straight, said he was just standing by the river staring at the *Cutty Sark.*

'Thanks,' said Coffin over the telephone to Bernard Jones. 'I'll keep my eyes open for him myself. I think I know his face. Red hair with a matching moustache on Place, as I remember, and a bit of a bent nose.'

'You've got the man. And it was his wife who bent the nose. With her handbag. Like father, like daughter.'

Bernard Jones was his hot line to what was happening inside Greenwich; it was always useful to have one, especially as he himself had more than one case on his hands. Crime was really bubbling in South London.

His career was at an interesting point. He had recently been appointed to head a small group of detectives based in South London and charged with the overall investigation of all serious crimes in the area. The Tactical Activity Squad it was called, known as TAS. It was a period when such bodies bearing impressive initials were appearing on all sides. He and TAS were a part of the times. He was assisted by a chief inspector, who was his deputy, and by a very young and sharp inspector, and by three even younger detective-sergeants. He found himself relying more and more on Inspector Paul Lane. The authority of TAS overrode the local CID structure, which had lately been the subject of an inquiry. He was well aware that he and his team were not popular and that to see him rubbed out by a man of known violence would cause very few tears.

'Thanks, Bernard. What about a drink at the Painted Parrot at the weekend?' An arrangement was made. It was Wednesday and he was home early for once.

He went to look out of his window. Not very likely that either Egan or his son-in-law, Terry Place, would be walking down Church Row, but you never knew. His luck might be in.

Round the corner from Queen Charlotte's Alley came a girl, tall and slender, with bright auburn hair tied in a ponytail with a white bow; she was pushing a pram and was accompanied by a young boy who was holding her hand. He was hanging on to the skirt of a small girl. Behind them came a youth, also red of hair, clearly related, carrying a bundle.

There was something about that bundle that looked familiar to John Coffin.

The whole procession came to a stop outside No. 5. Then the lad approached the house, and he heard the bounding of feet up the stairs and the noise of something bouncing against his front door.

He counted up to ten, then went to look.

Yes, his washing. The girl pushing the pram was Sarah Fleming. She had a bright, clever face, with the promise of beauty, she looked about sixteen, but was no doubt older. Her clothes were simple, jeans and a shirt, but she wore them with style. Style, yes, that was it, she had style.

And if the rest of the bunch, the little ones, were not her own offspring, then they were her brothers and sisters.

QUEEN CHARLOTTE'S ALLEY was a short cul-de-sac bounded at the end by Deller's soap factory. Deller's no longer made soap on the premises; thus the air was not so noisome as previously, but it was still a working concern with heavy lorries rumbling in and out of the yard all day. Queen Charlotte's Alley was not a quiet street, and never had been throughout its two hundred years of life, because the little workmen's cottages had housed the large families of the times, many of whom had worked in the foundry which had stood on the site where Deller's was built. In those days there had been access straight through from the alley.

Now there was only one large family in the street and that was the Flemings. The other houses, and there were but six, were nearly all occupied by young couples who liked to say they had bought an eighteenth-century house in Greenwich and were renovating it. Which usually meant putting in a new kitchen and a bathroom and brass fittings on the front door. There were a couple of elderly survivors from the old days, living on in their unreconstructed cottages. The Fleming family belonged in this party since the house had been rented by the family for at least three generations. To their despairing landlord they seemed like sitting tenants in perpetuity.

'I don't like you doing his washing.'

'Oh fiddle. The money's good.' She was more or less working her way through the Polytechnic A-levels course, with a firm eye on Oxford. She was bright and knew it. 'Old Brocklebank did us a good turn. Besides, I only take it down the launderette, and then iron it. He could do it himself if he thought about it.' From John Coffin she had earned enough money to buy two books she badly wanted: she created a kind of study for herself in a corner of the kitchen, with a table and bookshelves where she could work in peace. Like everything Sal did, it had a kind of imaginative elegance.

Now she was setting the table for a meal, moving briskly about. A kettle was humming on the old gas stove with a big brown teapot hung over the spout to get warm. In a little while there was toast on the table, a pot of jam, and a row of six cups to fill.

'Call the kids.'

'We're here waiting, Sal,' said a soft small voice.

'Yes, you are, Weenie, but not the others.'

Weenie was the little girl whose skirt had been so firmly grasped. Food was Weenie's delight, she was always hungry.

'They're under the table, Sal.'

Weenie lifted the cloth to reveal her three brothers crouched there. Their ages went up in steps. Then there was a big gap until Sal and her sibling, Peter. Mr Fleming had been away at sea for a good spell after their birth, then he came back and the family progression started again. Mrs Fleming never seemed to get the hang of birth control, to Sal's fury. Even in those days, she had known what would be best for the family. Less of them, far less. Preferably just her and Peter.

At the table, watching them eat, she felt this even more strongly. They were a responsibility.

'You certainly eat well, Weenie, but you don't grow on it.'

Something had gone wrong with the genes, she felt, when it came to Weenie and the others. She and Peter were all right. She knew herself to be clever and there were times when she felt beautiful, and Peter was certainly good to look at and he was very practical if not scholastically inclined. But the others, well, it was hard to be sure, she was watching them and trying to make up her mind. Not like me, she felt.

She knew she was doing what was right, but she didn't have to like it. The little ones could go into care, the social worker had said when their parents died, but Sarah had turned this down. It wasn't that she loved them so much, probably she didn't, but she had the feeling that there was something strange and secret about them as a family that was better kept private. So a special arrangement had been made with the social services.

'Give me some money,' she had said, 'we've got the house. We'll manage, thank you.'

They were a burden she had hoisted on her own back and it was heavy there.

Weenie, Tom, Lester, and Eddy.

'Where have you boys been putting your feet? Black marks all over the carpet,' she said, then pressed on without waiting for an answer. 'Your turn tomorrow,' she said to Peter. 'I'm at the Poly.'

She had had to leave school before her A-levels, but she was continuing her studies at the local Polytechnic College. It was her intention to get a place at Oxford. Balliol, she believed, would suit her as it seemed a radical place. She was left-wing in her politics.

He grunted assent; he never argued with her.

'The Pitts are back,' he said. By which he meant he would rather be with them than her, wanted to be invited by them and hadn't been.

'I noticed.'

'Nona's home.' But he hadn't seen her. That was what he meant.

'Three years is a long time, Pete.' A long time for a girl like Nona; she had been twelve when the two had been inseparable and Peter only fifteen. Now she was fifteen, nearly sixteen. She would have changed. Sal knew how a girl could change. Especially a girl with Nona's background. But Peter had not changed. People like Peter don't. They become what they have it in them to become at an early age and stay that way. Possibly for ever.

'You couldn't expect things to be the same.'

'It was her mother's fault. I blame her. Everyone knows she was having an affair with that MP. And because Mr Pitt was angry he took it out on me.'

It hadn't been the way it was, and she thought he knew it, but she could sympathize with his anger. Compared with the Pitts, what did he have?

'Nona was only a kid,' was all she said.

He was silent. Then he said: 'That chap you're doing the washing for is a policeman.'

'I know.'

It was the only thing she had against him.

John Coffin, policeman, was not someone she wanted to work for. Why couldn't he be a dustman or a bank clerk?

THERE WAS a telephone call for John Coffin when he got home from work that night. He was early, for once, and the telephone sounded within minutes of his arrival, as if it had been ringing at intervals hoping to get him.

'John? Bernard here.' The sergeant's voice was urgent. 'There's been a body found. You'll hear about this through channels, but I'm telling you now. I don't know how you'll get the message but take it seriously. If I were you I'd get down there now and see what they've got. Go through the Wolsey Road entrance to the Park.' And he rang off.

A green and wooded hill stretches down Greenwich Park towards the river. The ground is uneven with many little dips and hollows. The body of Malcolm Kincaid, the suicide, had been found in one such. John Coffin had walked home that way after parking his car in the garage he rented. He enjoyed the walk but felt alone on it, undressed. Every other walker seemed to have either a dog or a child. Perhaps he might get a dog. Except for his sister Laetitia, his life was empty of close personal relations at the moment. Laetitia, a long-lost sister who had come back into his life some years ago, was a joy. But she was rarely in the same country he was or indeed in any country for long. As well as a rich and itinerant husband, she had a successful career as a lawyer which seemed to involve a great deal of travelling.

There was their other sibling, of course, related by half blood through their mother to them both. But at the moment he or she was more hypothetical than real because they had not managed to track him down. Or her. It was strange to think that his mother had given birth to yet another child about whom he had known hardly anything until Laetitia had told him. But she had their mother's word for it. 'Born between you and me and given for adoption,' Laetitia had said.

Their mother seemed to shed children like lost parcels.

As he had walked down the hill towards Church Row he had seen a police car speeding up the hill. Trouble somewhere, he had thought, dragging his feet free from a patch of wet tarmac that lay across the pavement. Now he knew what it meant and where to go.

In through the gate, along the path towards the chestnut walk, always the ground rising. A small crowd of people standing watching from a distance, barriers being put into position and the whole area cordoned off.

Yes, he was here in good time.

He was known; his rank and his position smoothed the way.

Among the trees was a thicket of shrubs with a small path which led to a tiny brick pavilion with a bench in it.

Crouching against the bench as if he was praying was the figure of a man. His back was towards Coffin.

He walked right up to him and stared in the dead face. Eyes open, mouth twisted.

'Good Lord.' Not the face he had expected.

'Know him, sir, do you?'

Oh yes, I know him, and you know I know him.

'It's Billy Egan.' William Howard Egan, who had come out of prison eager to revenge himself on those who put him there. His son-in-law first and then John Coffin. Or possibly the other way round; on that point one had never been quite sure.

And now he was dead himself. Only a few weeks out of prison and murdered.

He looked as though he had been garrotted: there was blood in his mouth and coming out of his ears. Even bloody tears around his eyes.

But in addition, he had been stabbed many times. Cut and slashed as by a madman.

'I supposed we ought to start looking for Terry Place,' said Coffin.

On his way home he saw that the steps of No. 22 had been newly washed. Mrs Brocklebank at it again, he thought.

TWO

TERENCE PLACE was certainly to be looked for, but he was nowhere to be found. The police investigation into the death of Billy Egan slithered around, not taking hold anywhere. Egan had been first strangled with a tight cord, then stabbed repeatedly. The knife had not been found. But one peculiar fact emerged from a study of Egan's clothes. He had mouse droppings in his jacket pocket.

Meanwhile the Pitt family held its Welcome Us Back party to which everyone who was invited went and quite a few who were not.

John Coffin attended, but he was among those asked. For years afterwards he regarded it as one of the best parties he had ever been to. Even taking into the account all the things he later perceived as springing from it. The reason he found it such a good party was that no one there, apart from his host and hostess (but with one exception), knew that he was a policeman. There was no denying that if you were known to be a policeman the conversation became stilted and full of boring jokes, all of which he had heard many times before. He resolved to be anonymous ever after. The other reason was that there he came across his half-sister Laetitia; she was the exception, of course.

She came into the room in company with a well-known back-bencher MP.

He ought not to have been surprised to see her, after all the Pitts were part of the world she moved in. He knew she'd been living in New York. He was not at all surprised not to see her husband with her. Marriage was a movable feast to his sister.

'Nice to see you,' he said, giving her a kiss. 'But surprised.'

'I came because I hoped you'd be here.' A kiss from her in return and a breath of what he guessed to be the newest scent. 'You know Chris Court?'

'By name, of course.' He might have said by reputation, because he thought he knew something of that too. Christopher Court was a clever and energetic man who was known to be ambitious to lead his party. His friends said he might do it, if he could keep clear of scandals. He had fallen into minor trouble once or twice.

'I'm kind of a gatecrasher here. Chris was coming anyway and I asked him to bring me along.' She spoke with the supreme confidence of one who had never been unwelcome anywhere. 'But I knew Eddie and Irene in New York, of course.'

The Pitts occupied the whole of No. 22, all three floors, whereas most of the other houses in Church Row had now been subdivided into flats such as that into which John Coffin had now settled. The party was being held in a large ground-floor room which opened into the garden, where a few guests were already strolling.

Laetitia's confidence was justified. She was received with a cry of delight from her hostess, who pointed out where Edward Pitt was and said he would 'just love to see you'. Laetitia looked as if she knew it. She was wearing a cream silk pleated dress with a long rope of pearls; Irene was floating in chiffon of ivory and ice-cream colours; the two women matched, as if somehow they were meant to stand together and be photographed. But Irene moved away with Christopher Court while Laetitia stayed talking with her brother.

'Come into the garden?'

'Too cold. Damp as well. I'm not as English as you are, John. English gardens are all right to look at, but not to take a drink in.'

'I call it quite warm tonight.'

'Exactly what I mean.'

They were standing by a great gilt wall mirror in which all the room was reflected. The room was part library with one wall entirely covered with books. An ebony stand with a cascade of flowers filled one corner, and in another corner was a bronze head of Irene on a similar stand. Through an open door into another room he could see Mrs Brocklebank carrying a platter of food towards a table. The boy helping her and the tall young creature behind, also carrying food, must be the Pitt son and daughter.

Chris Court and Irene were standing at the door to the garden, poised as if they might walk out. Irene always looked gracefully ready for movement, like the dancer she might have been; she had a natural elegance, with her sculptured profile and creamy skin, which she had groomed and refined to a beauty it might not otherwise have possessed. Above all, she looked intelligent and alert.

They were talking softly, but audibly.

'It's been a long time.'

'Three years. What I promised Edward.'

'I kept my word. Didn't try to see you. Although I wanted to. By God, I wanted to. Now Edward's retired and the bargain is called in. We're free.'

Irene did not answer. She was staring into the garden. Then she turned to Christopher. 'Anything to tell me on that business of the student that I asked you to find out about?'

'Not yet. There will be. I've put my chap on to it. I can't see why you are worried, though.'

'It's because she didn't say anything. Ever. Not to me, not to her father. That alarms me. Come into the garden.'

And in the mirror Coffin watched Edward watching them.

He turned to Laetitia with a question in his eyes. She shrugged.

'So that's really why you came? You're a kind of a chaperon.'

'I'm very fond of both Chris and Irene. Edward too, for that matter. And also,' she added deliberately, 'of my brother whom I came to see, and who never comes to see me.'

'Poor coppers can't travel the globe finding you.'

But it was an excuse, and he knew it. He had not tried hard enough. She had a right to be angry if she wanted to be. He had got stuck into his own life, his own problems, and had not looked outside them.

'I'm coming back to this country to settle. Bought a house on Chelsea Embankment, with views across the river.'

Did it mean another marriage was unfastening itself? She did step out of relationships so easily. She was more like their mother than he cared to admit.

'How's Harry?'

'He will be there too.' She smiled. 'You thought not, didn't you.'

'Wondered.'

'There is a reason. Can't you guess? I am going to have a child. Since I was born in this country I have kept my British passport; my child, if born here also, will have dual nationality, British and American. We thought it a good idea he should be born here.' She was serenely sure of herself. 'The place not to be born if you are a boy is France, then you have to do military service, whoever you are. Or keep out of the country. And that might seriously damage his career. One can't tell.'

He was pleased. His family was growing. Now there would be three of them and a hidden fourth. 'It is a he? You are sure?'

'I already know. It is quite possible to know.'

Her life was so much more sure and full of certainties than his own was. That had to come from her father's side of the family. Nothing like it seemed to exist on what he knew of his mother's. He didn't know much about his own father, except that he had been an unlucky chap. It had been a surprise when Laetitia had turned up in his life, so much younger, prettier and cleverer than he had dared to expect. Also a woman; he had been on the search for a brother. That brother still existed somewhere.

'Of course, I am already a little old for a first child,' she said calmly. 'One can run into trouble, hence all the tests. But all is well.'

A budget of news.

When he turned back into the room, now crowded with people, he saw that Chris Court and Irene Pitt had drawn apart, the MP to talk to a man John Coffin recognized as a television personality, and Irene to supervise the laying out of the food in the other room. His sister was talking to Edward Pitt, who was giving her some wine, then going on to pour some for Court. He did it with a flourish.

Suddenly Coffin felt sorry for the man. Not much fun to lose your wife after years of marriage. If I was him, he thought, I'd feel like dropping poison in Court's drink.

Of course you'd have to choose your poison, or someone like himself, some eager beaver policeman, would soon be on your trail.

He enjoyed the party, but left early. His sister had left even before he did. She came across to speak to him before she went.

'Can I drive you home, Letty?' They were, after all, well out in South London, well away from Cheyne

Walk. He felt sure her new house was on Cheyne Walk, nothing less would do for Laetitia.

'No, I have a car.'

'Sure?'

'I am perfectly fit,' she said firmly. 'Don't fuss. There's something I want to say. You remember the advertisements we have been running in the papers asking about our missing sibling?'

'I remember.' He hadn't wanted the advertisements inserted, it was making public something he still preferred to keep private, but he had deferred to her.

'We've had an answer. Some woman who thinks she may know something. From Glasgow, of all places. Can one of us really have got to Glasgow?'

'You got to New York.'

'But I had help.' She questioned. 'So what do we do? Do we go to Glasgow?'

'One of us ought to.'

'Then I will send you the letter and all the information I have. I think you will find it interesting.'

As he followed her to her car he saw that Court was already standing by it with the door open.

'He's in a hurry, isn't he?'

'There's a Division tonight. A three line whip, he has to get back to the House to vote. Besides, better not to hang around.'

'Perhaps he'd have done better still not to come.'

Letty shrugged. 'There's something worrying you. What is it?'

'I've got a nasty murder case boiling up,' Coffin admitted. 'It's on my mind a bit.' He told her about the discovery of Egan's body, just hinting at his personal involvement.

'Is it a very horrible murder?' She knew that there were certain types of killing that he found hard to stomach.

'Bad enough. But I've known worse.'

'Then is it you don't know which way to go? You have no idea who did it?'

'Oh I think we do. Probably won't be too hard to prove, either.'

'Then you're home. It's at an end.'

Slowly Coffin said: 'That's just it. It doesn't feel like the end. More like a beginning. And I've got the nasty feeling that it's not the right murder.'

'You mean the wrong man was killed.'

'No, I'm sure the killer meant to get Egan. If he hadn't, Egan would have got him.'

'Well, then.'

'Yes, I know I'm being unreasonable.'

He saw her drive off, then made to leave himself. It was a warm evening for the time of year, with a big yellow moon hanging in the sky. He stood for a moment on the doorstep enjoying the evening. The noise from the party floated out to the street, laughter and happy voices mixed with the sound of music. A good party but now was the time to leave it, you should always leave a party while it was still happy. A good recipe for life.

He walked down the street. Just for the moment he fancied he could get a whiff of the old Deller's smell, but that must be fantasy. Deller's, once the boast of the district, had not smelt for over ten years now, vanquished, as it had been, by the Clean Air Act.

It was a night for memories and he had plenty centred on this district. A mixed bag, as memories tend to be, but all of them worth hanging on to. That was something he had learnt over the years, that painful memories could be very valuable, marking a place in your life where you had gone wrong but need not do so again.

As he got to his front door he looked back. To his surprise he saw the tall Fleming boy, he thought Mrs Brocklebank had told him he was called Peter, standing across the road from No. 22.

Poor lad, he thought. Listening to the party, but not of the party. Hearing the gaiety but not invited to it.

Then he saw a figure flit up the basement stairs and run across the road to the boy. He recognized the daughter of the house.

He let himself into the house and walked up the stairs, half sorry for the pair, half envious. Lucky young beggars, he thought. You've got it all to go through and it's a pain as well as a pleasure, but you'll miss it when it's done.

A bit later he took another look from the window. Yes, they were still out there under the street lamp. Just parting under the tree. The boy was hanging on to the girl's hand, letting go reluctantly, then slowly walking away.

Romeo and Juliet, no less, he thought.

WHEN THE PARTY was over Edward and Irene were alone in the kitchen, and both of them knew that something had to be said, was going to be said, but were reluctant to be the one who began.

'Sandwich?' Irene examined an open sandwich which still had its piece of smoked salmon adhering to it.

'No, thank you.'

'Just as well probably, it's drying out.' She put it aside. 'There's something unpleasing about a dried-out bit of smoked salmon, isn't there? Mrs B. didn't manage badly though. Good marks for her.'

'There's one thing you can't do, couldn't do in New York and can't do here where there's less excuse, and that's get good servants.'

'Mrs B.'s all right.' Irene was both surprised and defensive. It was not like Edward to be hostile. Or rude to her. Angry sometimes, yes, but not unpleasant.

'She's an old soak.'

'No, I don't think so.' Now Irene was really taken aback. 'Not her.'

'If the pile of whisky bottles I found neatly hidden away in the basement is anything to go by, she is. I don't know who else could have left them there.'

'The Leggetts...?' began Irene. 'We let them the house,' before she remembered what the Leggets, vegans and into yoga, were like. No, it couldn't be them. And anyway they would have left the bottles around. Hiding or even tidying up was not their style.

'No, I can see it would not be them. But I dispute Mrs B., I don't think she drinks at all.'

'Then she's got a boyfriend who does.'

'Edward! Why are you being so nasty? What's the matter with you?'

'Do you need to ask?'

'It's because Christopher came here.'

'Yes, I could have done without that. He wasn't asked. Or was he?'

'I sent an invitation,' admitted Irene. 'I wasn't sure if he'd come.'

'You were sure.'

'I knew we'd meet sometime. But we've kept our word. I agreed to wait for a divorce until you retired. You agreed.'

'I don't have to like it, though, and I don't have to like him. And I don't.'

'I hate you being like this.' Irene stood her ground, not giving anger back for anger, but she was unhappy. 'You seem less than yourself. Not worthy of what you are.'

'You don't really understand, do you?'

Irene shook her head silently.

'Ask Othello,' he said under his breath. 'He knew all about jealousy.'

Irene turned her head away. She shovelled all the unfinished food into the waste-bin. Who wanted to see cold sausages on sticks and soggy pastry with bits of caviare on it in the morning? And clearing up the mess of the party seemed the right and only thing to do in the circumstances.

Edward stood watching her, but not helping.

'Where's Nona?'

'In bed, I expect.'

'She's not. I just looked.'

'Around somewhere.' Irene was casual. She did not hang over her daughter.

'You're a lousy mother.'

'That's not true.' She was hurt. Not only was it not true, but Edward had never shown signs of thinking it before.

'You ought to know where a child of fifteen is.'

'Nona is quite grown up.'

'All the more reason.'

Irene said nothing, just pushed some more rubbish from the party into the bin.

'There's been a murder around here, you know.'

'I do know. Mrs Brocklebank told me.'

'I don't want Nona out on her own after dark.'

'She's not likely to be killed.'

'Don't even say it.'

Then they both heard the careful, quiet closing of the front door.

Nona came into the room, then stopped in surprise. She had returned home expecting them to be in bed. She would certainly have preferred them to be. She had long had her own ways of entering and leaving No. 22 in private, she remembered them from of old. Which to her meant before New York.

'Hello.'

She was taller than her mother, with Irene's dancer's grace turned to athleticism, but she was going to be just as beautiful in a more extrovert way, with a kind of flourish to her that Irene had not. She was very thin at the moment because she hated the idea of putting on weight. Muscles curved gently beneath her skin and she distrusted them also. That was not the way she wanted to go. 'Hello. Still up?'

'Where have you been?'

'Oh Dad! I'm allowed out, you know. Do I have to say?' She looked from parent to parent. 'Oh, all right. I was talking to Peter.'

Edward relaxed. 'I don't mind you being with him. He's a nice boy. Not very clever, not particularly well educated, but a nice lad.'

'You told me never to see him again before we went away last time,' said Nona, who did not forget easily.

'That was then. You were only a child.'

'And this is now?' Nona had an adult amusement in her eyes. Her mother saw it, and made her own assessment.

'Haven't you outgrown him?' she asked. 'I thought you might have done.' She understood her daughter better than her husband did, had watched her and seen the signs.

'I was kind of saying goodbye,' said Nona. 'Of course, I'll go on knowing him, he'll always be my friend. But, well, I've got a lot of work in front of me if I'm going to get to Girton or it might be Vassar, I haven't decided. I'm not going to have the time to go around much. And then I've just got keen on painting. I want to go to all the galleries, and look. The National, and the Tate and the Victoria and Albert. I don't think Peter would want to trail around all those after me. Not his thing.'

'No,' said Irene. How grown-up she was, how wise and sophisticated. Aware that two worlds had grown wide apart and it was time to be off. And how much wiser than she herself had been at that age. A wise child now but still one who had to be protected. It was better if she kept away from the boy. If only she had told me, Irene thought, and not allowed me to find out from a teacher's report. That made it important. An episode like that in a child's life ought to have been talked about. 'Well, be careful how you do it, that's all. Don't hurt his feelings.' More than you can help; they were going to be hurt, anyway.

'Your mother will teach you how to say goodbye gently,' said Edward, just audibly.

Irene heard him but said nothing. Bridges were being torn down, but would have to be built again. Somehow.

Nona said, 'Oh, I'm being slow about it. We're going out for a walk in the park. He wants to show me the sailing ship, the *Cutty Sark*. That'll be interesting. And did you know there had been a murder? A man, stabbed to death.'

She was interested but untouched. Death, violent death, was so far away from her.

LATER THAT NIGHT, Chris Court was on the telephone to his party agent in his constituency. The vote that night had not gone well for the Government and it was likely that there would be a General Election.

Chris's seat was one which, if the swing was large, would be marginal. He had worries.

As they finished their business, Chris said carefully, 'I think there might be a divorce coming up. I'll be involved. Of course there's no question of anyone being labelled a guilty party these days, but will it matter, do you think?'

'No,' said his agent confidently. 'Just try and get it well over before the Election.'

'Yes. Right.' He would have to talk over the dates with Irene, but she would be reasonable. 'It's my second divorce, you know.'

'That's all right. A friend of mine is agent for a chap who's just about to have his fourth. In the Labour Party, too. That's trouble. But he'll probably get in all the same. The voters aren't what they were.'

He was always optimistic, a bouncy man, like a cuddly bear with hidden claws, able to override worries; he would not be a political agent otherwise.

'By the way, that inquiry you wanted me to make for you, about the missing students. I put one of your research assistants on to it, the little Scot, Fiona Graham, and she picked up something in the local paper down there in Greenwich. Yes, there was a story about three students but nothing much to it, they weren't really missing, soon turned up and it never made the London papers. But she did pick up the story that one of the same students was later found dead. A keen little researcher, our Fiona. Suicide, but a bit of puzzle because they never found the poison. Or the bottle. Or something like that.'

'Thanks, yes, that is a help. I just wanted to know what there was in the story.'

'A something and nothing. Want Fiona to go on?'

'No.'

'I'd try the police if I were you. There seems to have been a feeling they knew a bit more than they were saying. They had an idea a child was involved somewhere. If it's that important.'

'Someone wanted to know.'

'Otherwise I'd leave it alone. It's always dangerous digging up old stories.'

He spoke out of a full knowledge of the world, but without expecting anyone to believe him and without any certain information to go on.

Although it was late, Chris sat by his telephone waiting for the call, and when it came he answered it quickly and quietly, as if it mattered his end as much as it did the other.

'Irene? Yes, there was a child involved. But I don't know any details.' He listened. 'Yes, love, I'll try. And you try not to worry, I think you are fancying things.'

He really believed what he said.

LATER THAT NIGHT, John Coffin was still up and reading, when his bell sounded. He listened on the entryphone.

'Oh, Paul, come on up.' He released the front door and waited. In a short while he heard feet on the stairs and opened his door. 'You're around late.'

Inspector Paul Lane was shorter than the ideal height for a policeman but compensated for it by a solid square frame and hard muscle that made his ability to look after himself never in doubt. He was young for an inspector and wrote a very good report, the product, no doubt, of having taken a sound degree in history at York University. He was reputed to have a very happy marriage, but if so, his wife was a patient woman who made do with not much of his company, because he was always working. As now. This was no casual call.

'I saw your light was on.'

Since Church Row was not on any route that Paul Lane might have been taking to home or work, there had to be more to it than a social conversation. Coffin waited.

'Nice to see you. Have a drink? This is whisky, but you could have anything.' He thought about what he had apart from water and orange juice and probably a can of beer in the refrigerator.

'Any coffee?' Lane put down his briefcase.

'If I open a jar.'

Lane pulled a face. 'You ought to learn how to cook.'

'I've never been able to notice the difference between one sort of coffee and another.'

'That's because you don't treat the stuff properly. I bet you open a packet and then leave it around going stale for weeks. I'll take the whisky.'

After a moment of silence, he said, 'We've found a bike. That is, a lad exercising his dog found it dumped in some bushes in a park around an old people's home in Charlton. It's always a boy with a dog, isn't it? He shouldn't have been there, of course, with his dog and it's not clear why he was, looking for his grandfather, he says, but his grandfather doesn't live there, is only thinking he might go in one day. Anyway, the lad found the bike the day before yesterday and told his dad and they went out and wheeled it home. After a closer inspection, they decided they didn't like the look of it and that it might not be the bit of buckshee good luck they'd thought at first. So the man told a pal of his who was a copper. He took it to the local nick. After a bit, it occurred to them there that it might be of interest to us.' Lane took a long drink. 'It had a lot of blood on it, you see. All over. The boy had taken it for rust, but the father knew it for what it was.'

'The blood group?'

'Same as Egan's. It has to be his. The killer used the bike to get away.'

'Could be,' observed Coffin moderately. 'They took their time letting us know. Malice deliberate, do you think?'

Lane shrugged. 'No, just a natural slowness. They don't love us, though.'

'I think we were created as a group because someone hated us.' Coffin was half serious. He had enemies as well as friends. If he failed in what he was doing, bringing up to efficiency this whole sluggish CID area, then his career could be at a dead end. But he had picked his team deliberately and well. 'Any fingerprints on the bike?'

'Place is too cunning a bastard for that.'

'If it is Place that killed Egan.'

But they both thought it was. He had disappeared from public view and his contacts and such friends as he had were keeping silent.

'Until we are sure let's call him X,' said Coffin. 'Any forensics?'

'Still waiting. But with my naked eye I saw a bit of cloth caught in the saddle bar. Also a shred of plastic in the handlebars. The killer could have had a bag there, with the knife in it. We haven't found the knife; he's probably got it.'

'Pity he didn't leave it with the bike,' said the still sceptical Coffin. 'If the bike was all over blood he must have been covered with it himself. Quite a sight riding through the streets.'

Paul Lane ignored this sally. 'It was late at night. And I don't suppose he went out of his way to meet people. Either coming or going. And we have got a bit from the forensics. About Egan himself. There were shreds of grass on his shoes.'

'So he walked to his rendezvous in the park. He'd have to do that. Even Egan. Not much of a walker, our William, as I remember.'

'There were also traces of asphalt, or some sticky, tarry stuff on the soles and uppers of his shoes. It looks as though he'd tried to rub it off with a bit of newspaper and hadn't succeeded.'

'Yes, he always was a dressy man. Well, all the pavements around here seem to be under repair.' Coffin looked down at his own shoes. Even Church Row.

'Not all, but quite a few around the park,' said Lane in that reasonable voice that could infuriate his peers.

'I think he may have walked to his meeting. And if he did that, then he must have been hiding out somewhere not too far away. Not being, as you rightly say, much of a walker.'

'Could be.'

'So we might be able to find out where that was.'

There was silence between the two men as they considered William Egan coming out of his hiding place and then walking to meet his death.

'The time of death has finally been agreed upon as about midnight,' said Lane, coming across with another piece of information. 'The medical lot didn't want to come across with that yet, still doing tests on the gut or something, but I prised it out of them. The park is locked by that time, but I can think of at least three ways of getting in, and if I know them then Egan knew them.'

'I wonder who issued the invitation to that particular meeting? And how it was set up?'

'When we know that we will know the lot.'

'If I know Egan and his son-in-law there was either a woman or money in it.'

'A bait? Yes. I'd put Egan as the inviter. It has his mark on it somehow. But he walked into something he didn't expect. He walked and X cycled. That makes them both living locally.'

'Yes, I can accept that. If the bike is right,' added Coffin cautiously.

'That was my patch once, remember,' said Lane.

'I know.' The bright boy from Guildford Grammar School and York University had started his career in the Force in an unsmart part of South London.

'Where the bike was found is not far from where X's sister lived.'

'Why are we still calling him X? We both know we mean Place. I give you best on that. I think you are right,' said Coffin. 'But it's still guessing.'

'I went to call on his sister. Went to her house in Abinger Road. Just dropped in. I took as much of a look round as I reasonably could. He wasn't there, of course.'

'That would have been lucky.'

'But he had been there. I swear it. I could almost smell him.'

'Perhaps he was still there.'

'No, I don't think so. There's not many places to hide in those little houses.'

He paused. 'And there's something else, something that worries me. His sister was frightened. She's a tough little body, Roxie Farmer, but she was really scared stiff.'

The two men looked at each other.

'You're thinking of the way Egan was cut up,' said Coffin slowly. 'I wondered about that myself.'

'Terry Place is either high on drugs or else he's gone off his rocker. Perhaps both. He's dangerous. His sister knows it and I reckon we know it.'

'Then we'd better find him fast.'

'He's living locally,' said Paul Lane. 'I swear it.' He bent down to get a package. 'I found this rolled up in a cupboard in the Farmer house. I persuaded his sister to let me take this tweed coat away. She didn't want me to have it, but it looked to me as if it matched the scrap of cloth caught on the saddle of the bike. I think it is Place's. I believe there is blood on it.'

He was holding out an old grey tweed jacket which had seen better days. It was wrapped in a big plastic bag to protect any evidence. There were dark stains up the front and on the sleeves.'

'Mad to leave it around.'

'I think he might be mad. Or near enough. But in any case, he might not have expected me to go to Abinger Road.'

'Any mice about? Egan had mice droppings on him.'

'I don't think they had Egan in Abinger Road. And from what I know of Roxie Farmer, no mouse would stand a chance. No, Place didn't have him there.'

'I suppose I ought to be grateful to him for killing Egan, seeing Egan was after me,' said Coffin.

'I found this in the pocket.' Lane held out a scrap of paper enclosed in a plastic envelope. He had done that himself. Standard practice. 'It'll have to be tested for traces. But he's got your address on it.'

Coffin studied it. The piece of paper had been much folded so that the pencil scrawl was hard to read, but he could make out Church Row well enough. 'That's Egan's writing.'

'I think so.' Lane nodded.

'So he knew where I was.'

'And now Place knows. Took this off Egan's body, and he meant something by that.'

'I hope I'm going to go on being grateful,' said Coffin grimly. 'Got anything else, or is that the lot?'

'There is this ticket to the *Cutty Sark*. He's been there, and quite recently too. He's always loved the river. He'll be down that way now. I'll take a bet on it.' He spoke with the utter conviction of someone who knew he was right. 'Why don't we look for him down there?'

Paul leaned forward and became urgent. 'Why don't we pour men in? Flood the place with searchers. Flush him out quick.'

'Going to take a lot of overtime,' said Coffin, somewhat sourly. You always had to think about money now.

But they agreed to try. If they could get the manpower. The TAS squad was small and its demands not welcome. But it could be done.

'Leave that stuff with me,' said Coffin, motioning towards the jacket and the paper in its plastic envelope. 'I'll take responsibility.'

Coffin saw his visitor to the front door. As he closed it behind Lane and walked up the stairs he had the feeling he got sometimes that wheels were moving. It was never a wholly pleasant feeling, unsettling and worrying.

Mrs Brocklebank would have called it ghosts, the spirits operating. But Coffin recognized it as human relationships interlocking and interacting and setting the machine in motion.

When you thought about it, it all came down to people.

He picked up the piece of paper again and held it to the table lamp. 'Wait a minute. I didn't look at this properly before and neither did Paul. Paul misled me and he misled himself. Not my address here. My number is 5 . . .'

He looked again. He could just make out that there was a faint number written there.

'No. 22.'

THREE

THE MURDER CASE slipped easily into its next phase, as if it had been programmed by a computer that had access to several personal files and knew where they interacted.

Coffin was still pondering on the significance of what he had seen written on the piece of paper from Place's jacket. He had sent jacket and paper off to the laboratories, demanding an instant report. This had arrived and a copy had been sent to Inspector Lane. As far as they could tell, the writing, by a ballpoint, was Egan's. The paper was of poor quality and had been torn off a pad of the kind you might keep in a kitchen or by a telephone. In Place's pocket it had picked up fluff and minute scraps of human skin and hair. It had both Egan's fingerprints on it and those of Place, blurred but identifiable.

At the same time a determined police search for Terry Place began in the area down by the river. It was neither quiet nor unobtrusive, since it was not intended to be. The aim was to frighten Place into acting hastily. Within a further twenty-four hours, his sister, Mrs Roxie Farmer, divorcee, was taken in for questioning at Royal Hill police station, but claimed she knew nothing. In spite of an on-slaught by Inspector Paul Lane, she gave nothing away.

That is, until the very end of the interview. Lane had been assisted by a woman police officer, Detective-Sergeant Phyllis Henley, a thickset girl, whom he had called in because she was an old friend or enemy of Roxie whose own life had not been without criminal excitements.

On the table between the two police officers, in view of Roxie, lay the forensic report on the jacket found in Roxie's house.

'Come on now, Roxie, you know me.' Sergeant Henley prided herself on her power to prise out information by a mixture of persuasion and light bullying like the icing on a cake, and although this had never worked particularly well with Roxie in the past, this was no reason not to try it now.

Roxie stayed silent as if she was determined not to be cozened, but she shifted uneasily in her chair.

'You can trust me.' Roxie looked sceptical, but still said nothing, just another little fidget. 'If I say we know your brother has been with you, then you can believe we do know. And if I say we think you know where he is now, then you can believe we know that too.' It was a long speech for Sergeant Henley, who relied on smiles and sighs and significant silences. And then a snap. The snap came now. 'Roxie, you had a tweed jacket hanging in your hall and that tweed jacket was worn by him very recently.' She did not add that it had blood on it, although she knew that too, having just read the forensic report.

Roxie shrugged.

'Something sharp cut the pocket lining. Lost a kitchen knife, have you Roxie?'

Roxie looked sullen.

'Threaten you with it, did he, Roxie? Where's your daughter, Roxie? Sent her away, haven't you? Threaten her with the knife, if you talked, did he?'

Roxie found her voice. 'Shut up, you.'

Sergeant Henley gave the Inspector a quick triumphant glance. 'I think I could make a guess where your daughter is, and probably so could he. I know where your aunt lives. He's better caught. Tell us where he is then, Roxie.'

Roxie set her mouth firmly in silence. It looked like the edge of a knife itself.

Sergeant Henley said, without noticeable kindness: 'If I were you, Roxie, I'd get your daughter home. She'd be better off with you than that drunken aunt of yours. Mrs Bow, she is now, isn't she? Her husband's none too safe with little girls, or hasn't anyone told you that?'

After a short pause, Roxie muttered: 'Remember he's a little rat that likes a hole.'

'Oh, come on, that's not good enough. No puzzlers.' Paul Lane was cold. 'You say what you mean in plain English.'

Sergeant Henley said: 'Speak up, now. Or Uncle Bow might find himself doing a lifer for your Rosie.'

Roxie said suddenly. 'There's a tunnel down by the river. I don't know where. You'd have to find it. Greenwich Pier. He used to play in it years ago. In the war.'

Years ago, thought Paul Lane, I suppose it's still there. Well, she thinks it is, anyway.

'Thanks, Roxie,' he said, and pulled the telephone towards him.

When he had given his orders and they were alone, he said: 'You were rough on her, Phyllis.'

'But I got a result. And I'll tell you something else: what really frightened Roxie was that the kid might cooperate with Uncle Bow.'

Lane shrugged. He was never sure how to take his Phyllis.

'It's been known,' said Phyllis.

The message about the tunnel went to John Coffin, who got into touch with the Port of London Authority and the Greenwich Pier management for information and, better still, maps.

'No picnic, searching down there,' said the man at the end of the telephone. 'Do my best for you, but sometimes we don't know what we've got ourselves.'

NEXT MORNING in Queen Charlotte's Alley, Sarah Fleming was preparing a picnic for her brother Peter. She was doing so reluctantly, it was her Poly day and she really did not have time. The little ones, the very little ones, called it her 'Holy day', not distinguishing clearly between Poly and Holy. Sarah wondered if they were deaf in addition to other deficiencies. Growing deafer, moreover, as they had certainly not been deaf as babies. Putting all their energies into deafness rather than growing bigger and taller. It was the sort of fantasy she must not harbour.

'I've given you ham and cucumber. And there's a Thermos of coffee.'

'It ought to be smoked salmon and champagne for her,' said Peter. He was dressed ready for his outing in clean jeans and a white shirt. Sarah wore almost the same clothes, except that her shirt was red. A gesture to her political feelings.

'She's only a kid.'

'That's the sort of girl she is.' He saw himself as a great, strong animal who could always protect his girl. A bear?

'Count yourself lucky I didn't make you Marmite sandwiches.'

'There ought to be wine and music and a boat on the river,' he said dreamily.

'And you in a white tie and tails, I suppose.' They had recently watched an old Fred Astaire and Ginger Rogers film on the television in which she thought she saw the source of his fantasy.

'What about work? Aren't you going in?'

He had a part-time job in a large firm of chemists where he worked in the stockroom. There had been rumours of redundancies.

'Got the day off. Had it due. Sal . . . do you think I could do what you are doing? Work for my A's and then go to university?'

'Well, I've had my turn, only right you should have yours,' said Sarah judicially. 'I don't know about the little ones, though. I certainly can't take them to Oxford with me. I was relying on you.'

They both looked at their younger brothers and sister, who stared blankly back.

'I could take them out to the middle of a lake in a boat and drop them in. They can't swim. I have taken that precaution.'

'I never know when you are serious or not.'

'And I never know with you,' she answered.

There was a pause, broken by the girl.

'You'd have to stop playing games.'

'I don't play games.'

Sarah shrugged.

'I'd manage.' He looked hopeful. 'Fix something up. I might go to nightschool or something. Or the Open University.'

'You'd have to work at your grades.' His sister was at once more realistic and more perceptive. 'You've never been much of an exam passer.' Very poor, in fact, but no point in discouraging him. Another dream, though. He had so many. She saw him passing the day in a cloud of dreams.

'You mean why bother?' he said, seeing more than she had meant him to. 'I want to be as good as them, the Pitts. Look at what they are and what we are. What we've got and what they've got. It's not right. Things ought to be more equal.'

'We're what we are and they are what they are.' For various reasons, intellectual, historical and sexual, it was easier for her to accept things as they were than for Peter.

ROUND THE CORNER in No. 22, Church Row, Irene Pitt was watching her daughter prepare for a picnic.

'Sure you want to go?'

'Got to.'

Irene raised her eyebrows. 'That's not the way to enjoy yourself. If that's what you are going to do, of course.'

'I promised.'

'Is that a bottle of wine?'

'I thought we could use it.'

'Want any fruit? There's a pineapple in the refrigerator. Brie? I bought a nice wedge yesterday. Plenty if you want it. I'm going out to lunch myself.' With Chris, of course.

'Just the wine.'

They were in the kitchen, Irene still in a dressing-gown, an ivory frilled cotton to which she gave a golden glow, and Nona in jeans with a white shirt. Edward had gone off to see an editor at the BBC; he wanted to talk about a project on the Third World, and the boy was at school.

'How did you get the day off from school?' Irene slipped a few rich chocolates in a plastic bag and gave them to her daughter.

'The sixth form can work at home.' She looked at her mother. 'All right, this isn't work, but it's a good-bye session.' Or it would be, if she could get Peter to understand. 'I told you. So it's only once.'

Irene laughed. 'We always think that. It's not so easy saying goodbye.'

'Breaking things up? No, I know that. A lot of things are breaking up now.'

'You mean because of Chris and me. Do you mind? But that's silly. Of course you mind.'

'Yes, I do. Who will I stay with, you or Dad?'

'I suppose you will choose. You know that. We agreed.' The divorce had been talked over thoroughly in New York, or so she had thought. Now she wondered. But goodness knows, Nona had had her say there.

Nona looked around the kitchen. 'I might stay here. Just might. I'd want to go on seeing you a lot, though.'

'Thanks.'

'Don't be sharp. It's one of your worst things.'

'Is that why you've never told me about what happened with you and Peter before we all went to New York? Did you think I'd be sharp? I wouldn't have been. But I think you wanted me to know. You let me read that story you wrote for your class magazine: The Dragon's Mouth. That was really you and Peter finding that thing in the wood, wasn't it?'

'Might have been.'

'Might?'

'Was, then.'

'It frightened me that you had not told me. Made it important, very real.'

Nona shrugged.

'All the same, you didn't hand out many details. You made it a kind of fable. But there was a real incident. I know.'

Nona still kept quiet. 'I don't want to talk about it. I promised.'

Irene would have gone on, but for the arrival of Mrs Brocklebank.

She surveyed Nona and her preparation for a picnic. 'Off out? It's going to rain.'

'It won't rain.' Nona slung her bag over her shoulder. 'Thanks for the chocs. Anyway, we're going to see the *Cutty Sark.*'

'A lot of police down there. You're not supposed to see them, but you can. All over the place like rabbits.'

'Who cares?' Nona picked up the wine bottle, gave her mother a look and was gone.

Mrs Brocklebank had created a little nest for herself in the basement where she put her clothes and her big black handbag, from which she was only rarely and reluctantly parted, and where she tucked away any odds and ends it was better Brock at home did not see. Money was one. A woman was entitled to her own savings. She had such nests in every one of her working places, which her employers were only vaguely aware of. She had a kind of natural skill in camouflage.

Now she went to her corner next to which was a cupboard no one seemed to know about except Mrs Brocklebank, shared by her and a certain amount of animal life, and deposited her bag and coat. There was a small mirror hanging on the door in which she combed her hair; a woman liked to look her best even at work.

She was troubled and anxious. 'As though one death wasn't enough,' she said to herself. 'There's got to be others, by the look of it. And they say there's nothing wrong with this house and I'm imagining things.'

She had been a childhood friend of William Egan and though no one could truly mourn such a man of violence, still she had her loyalties, and he was a man who had known how to trade on them.

Later that day she would pop in, her words, to see Roxie Farmer in Abinger Road; she knew her too.

'Roxie,' she would say, 'every one of us has to look after their own. It's our duty, and you and I have done it. Me in my way, you in yours. But that Terry of yours has put himself beyond it. I reckon I know where he is as well as you do, and I might have to say. If he gets killed, he's got only himself to blame.'

All the same, she wished she had been stronger in her advice to Nona not to go down by the *Cutty Sark*. She had been too indirect, she should have said: Look, love, this is old Brocklebank speaking straight. It could be dangerous down there.

She got out her scrubbing brush. 'I'll just give the front step a scrub. I didn't like the look of it at all this morning.'

THE POLICE AND PICNICKERS converged upon the river. Peter and Nona were not the only people planning to eat in the open air, because a coachload of schoolchildren together with four teachers, all carrying packed lunches, had arrived to visit the *Cutty Sark* and then *Gypsy Moth* in its dry dock.

'Lot of people about. Too many.' It wasn't what Peter had had in mind when he thought of the picnic. Something more pastoral and solitary had been his vision.

'Some of them are policemen, I think. Mrs Brocklebank said so.' Nona looked about her with interest, trying to identify which of the young men in her vicinity could possibly be policemen. 'There has been a murder, you know. They are looking for clues, I suppose. And for the murderer.'

'I know. I don't want to talk about it.' He gripped her arm. 'Come on. There's a lot of things I want to show you.'

'Yes, and I want to see. I am very interested. I like objects, I've discovered that recently. But don't hold me so tight.'

He had once been the leader and she had been the unquestioning follower, but all that had changed now. Surely he could see it.

He did not seem to have heard. 'Quickly now. First the *Cutty Sark* and then we'll explore down by the river. Then our picnic on the hill by the Old Observatory.'

But when they were in the clipper Nona took a more detailed interest than he did. She was fascinated by the Saloon, set out for dinner with silver and glass; she hovered over the display of figureheads; but it was the rigging of the clipper that caught her imagination most. She stood at the foot of the mainmast, staring up at the intricacy of the complicated tracery of sails, spars and rope.

'You know why it is called the *Cutty Sark?*'

'Just a name.' Peter was not interested. 'Had to call it something.'

'It's from Robert Burns's poem *Tam o'Shanter.* It's about a witch who chased him on his mare. The Cutty Sark is the little shift or chemise the witch was wearing.'

'Funny name.'

'It probably comes from the French word *sacque,* that was a kind of loose blouse. It must mean the pronunciation was nearer to sark than sack.'

'Or at least in Scotland.' He turned away. He hated being instructed. 'Anyway, it's not a bad name for a ship. I suppose it means she went like a witch.'

The vessel was getting crowded now as another school party arrived. Nona would have lingered, looking at the fo'c's'le where the crew had slept, and the galley where the food was prepared, but he hurried her on.

'Let's go down to the pier. I want to show you something.'

The two of them were noticed and observed by at least two policemen. One was a young detective-constable, seconded from the Bromley district, who noticed Nona. He thought she was beautiful. He considered trying to make her acquaintance, but two things moved against it. First, he was on a job, and secondly, he knew without putting into words that she was no girlfriend for an ambitious copper. There was a third thing: he had caught sight of a superior officer: John Coffin.

Coffin was the other police officer who saw them. He gave the pair a friendly glance as they walked towards the riverside.

He was here checking up on the search for Terry Place. The feeling was the hunt was going well; they would find him.

Earlier that morning, speaking on the telephone, Paul Lane had said, 'With the number of men we have searching he can't get away. Not if he's in the area, and everything tells me he is.'

'He could stay in hiding a long while before we flushed him out.' No one knew better than John Coffin what a network of alleys, underground passages, and dark basements nestling in old buildings still lay near the river.

'Not the way I see it.' Lane had been positive in his usual clear-minded manner. One did not use the word cocky of such as Paul Lane, but it did cross Coffin's mind, if in no unfriendly spirit. He had been cocky himself once, and none the worse for it now. 'I'll keep in touch.' That was the other side of the coin with the Inspector. He might be strong in his own opinions but he did not go haring off on his own. He kept in touch.

A young plain clothes man touched his arm. 'Inspector Lane is looking for you, sir. He's over there in his car.'

Coffin turned his back to the pier, Peter and Nona had already disappeared down a flight of steps, and walked towards the road, where a line of police vehicles was drawn up.

Lane sprang out of the first car at his approach. 'We've got him, sir.'

'Good. Where?'

'Get in, and we'll go there. Forget the river. I reckon Roxie was leading us on there. Now we place him in a house. Up the hill, more towards Charlton way. Not down here by the river as we thought, after all. He always was a cunning beggar, and Roxie's another one.'

As the car travelled up the hill in Greenwich Park, Lane explained. 'He was sighted by a local man on the beat, was at school with him, is sure it's Terry.'

'You mean you haven't actually got your hands on him?'

'He was seen going into a house in Maryon Park Gardens. It's a street his sister admits he knew, had a girlfriend there. And he's not answering the door or coming out. It has to be Place.'

They drew up before one of the pair of red brick semi-detached houses in a street of other houses like it.

'And this is it?' Coffin studied the neat quiet house with a plot of garden in the front. 'Who's the house owner?'

'Neighbours say it's an old chap called Masterton. He's in hospital. He's had lodgers in and out.'

There was another police car at the kerb, with a woman sitting in the back. Coffin studied her face. She looked unhappy.

'That's Place's sister, Roxie Farmer. We got her down here.' He turned towards Coffin. 'So what now? Do we go in?'

'No.' Coffin sat back. 'Not yet. We wait.'

NONA AND PETER wandered by the river, with Peter pointing out the various features that interested him. Nona stared at the grey river where the wind was picking up little waves and throwing them against the walls of the river walk.

'Do you ever think about that thing that happened to us in the park? Before I went away. Do you think about it?'

'A long while ago now, Nona.'

'It was horrible.' She shivered.

'Animals die in the open air.' He stroked her arm. 'It's natural. Don't let it upset you.'

He was soothing her, but all the same there was excitement rippling through the muscles of his arm.

'You haven't spoken to anyone about it?'

'No. No, I haven't spoken to anyone.'

Not spoken, no. Told the whole world through a short story, if they wanted to read it.

Looking down at the river, she could see that the level had dropped, uncovering lines of bricks on the wall beneath them that looked as if they rarely saw the sun. The timber supports of the pier could be seen increasingly.

'Low tide.'

Peter nodded and drew her to the rail of the river-walk to look over the side. 'That's why I wanted us to get moving. I knew the tide would be on the ebb. And it's a very low tide now. Things get uncovered that you can't see easily at other times.' He knew about the river; in different times might have worked on it, happily and well.

He pointed to a dark patch to their left and very low down.

'See that door?'

She tried to make it out. 'Is there a door?'

'Doesn't look like one from here, but it is one. You'll see when we get closer.'

'Are we going to get closer?' She looked down at her white slippers, not fancying the mud and muck she could see there. Also, would they have to swim?

'There's a tunnel behind the door. It leads right up the hill into the park. I've heard that there's another door in the park somewhere, but I've never been able to find it. I spent hours looking when I was a kid.'

'What was the tunnel used for?'

Seriously, he said, 'I used to think for smuggling or for prisoners to escape. But I suppose really it was for supplies that came by ship to be carried to some of the houses on the hill, the Ranger's House, or the Observatory.'

'Is it used now?'

He shook his head, looking amused. 'Most people don't know anything about it.'

'You do, though.'

He nodded. 'I've been down there. It's good. Secret. Private.' He took her hand in his own warm, dry one. 'Come on. Let's go there now.'

'No. It looks wet and horrible. And I don't see how.' She tried to draw her hand away.

'Not wet at all,' he coaxed. 'Dry as a bone. And there's a little ledge to walk on. You won't get your feet wet. Or I could carry you.'

'If I come, then we won't stay long?' After all, she had entered on this day to please him. And she had said she wanted to see places of historical interest. He was only doing his bit.

'No, of course not. Then have our picnic.'

There was an iron gate which looked rusted and stuck but which opened to a touch, a flight of stone steps to the water level, and then she let herself be led along a narrow shelf which from the look of it was usually under water.

The entrance to the tunnel was a low wooden door. Tucked away unobtrusively in an angle of the river wall, it was also protected by a brick overhang. She could understand why most people did not know it was there.

'Do we have to go in? Anyway, it must be locked.' In spite of her best efforts there was a green stain on her white slippers. 'And damn, I've dropped the chocolates in the water.'

'Forget the chocolates, and the lock is broken. Come on.' He gave the door a strong push. With a creak it opened inwards on a dark hole. A breath of moist, yeasty air puffed out towards them.

'Thought you said it wasn't damp?'

'Look at the walls and floor. Dry as a bone.'

The walls were brick lined and the floor covered with dull tiles set in a herringbone pattern that reminded her of a Roman villa she had once seen near the South Coast. A small interest stirred inside her. Couldn't be Roman, of course, she could see that, but wasn't it interesting how traditional ways of doing things carried on?

'If you say so.' There were things that looked like ragged mushrooms growing out of the wall. On the other hand, the floor was dry.

Peter drew a torch out of his pocket and held it above his head; the beam spread out, eventually spending itself against the darkness of the tunnel. The path rose gently above water level and then bent to the left. Probably it went up the hill in a series of gentle planes. Carts might have been used to drag supplies up it, sufficient width was there.

'That's it, then.' She had seen enough and was ready to go.

'No, let's go inside. Just a bit. I've always wanted to go beyond that curve and I haven't liked to do it on my own.'

She gave him a sharp, surprised look. 'Why not?'

He shrugged. 'Don't know what's beyond. Better to have someone with you.'

He was a surprising boy. Imagination and nerves just when you did not expect it.

She took a few paces forward. 'What about rats?'

'If there are any, then they will be more frightened of us than we are of them.'

'Not true,' she said with conviction. 'I will be more frightened than they are.'

'Oh, come on. I'll keep any rats away.'

'I thought I heard something.'

'Let's take a look.' He was moving forward, and to keep in touch with him and the light from the torch she had to move too. 'We might find the other exit. No one's been here for years.'

'No?'

The air in the passage stirred and folded itself about her. She wrinkled her nose.

If no one had been here for years, why did she fancy she could smell cigarette smoke?

INSIDE THE HALL of the house in Maryon Park Gardens, a tearful, frightened little man was explaining that his name was Bill Pitkin, that he was not Terry Place, that he had never seen Terry Place nor ever heard of him. And, no, he had nothing to hide. The only reason he had not opened the front door had been because he was frightened. He did not know who was trying to break in.

FOUR

'AND OF COURSE, he does look like Place,' Lane admitted ruefully. 'Strong general resemblance. Not twins by any means, but close enough. And you can't blame him for being frightened. I frighten myself sometimes.'

He and John Coffin were standing in Maryon Park Gardens. Roxie Farmer was still sitting in the police car, looking out at them with an expressionless face. She wore a great deal of make-up at all times, but that day, perhaps just as primitive man might have painted his face as a protection, she was garnished with particularly bright eye colours and lipstick, so that it was a little garish mask staring at the two policemen. She saw the Chief Superintendent looking at her and turned her head away.

'Let's have a word with Roxie.' Coffin started to stroll towards the car. 'See what she can tell us. She used to be quite a truthful girl. In her own way.'

'You know her?' Lane was surprised.

'From the past. She was a case once herself, poor Roxie. Before your time.'

'What sort of case?'

'They call them battered babies now, I don't think we did then. But battered she was, the poor kid, and by her own father. Nearly killed her. They were a violent family. And Terry was her kid brother. For some reason he didn't get the kicks, but he certainly saw it happen.'

'It must have made an impression on you, that case,' observed the Inspector drily.

'I remembered the child's name: Roxie. It's an unusual one round here. We used to joke that she was named after a local cinema. Anyway, I was interested enough in Roxie to look the case up again... So let's go and talk to her now.'

'You won't get any more out of her, even if she remembers you.'

'She won't remember me or the episode. She was only a baby.' Or so he hoped. Be all there deep inside, though, he was sure of that as truth.

He got into the car beside her. 'Hello, Roxie, you won't remember me, but we met once.'

She stared silently, nothing welcoming in her face.

'You knew that wasn't your brother in that house. Why did you let us believe it could be?'

Roxie shrugged.

'Yes, silly question. You wouldn't help us if you could, would you? But did you help him? Your brother had a piece of paper in his pocket with Billy Egan's hiding place on it. That's what I think it is. And from the forensics, I believe Egan wrote it himself, perhaps to remember the address, and the paper somehow came into the hands of your brother so he knew where Egan was. Did you give it to him?' Roxie shook her head silently. 'Someone did. Your brother is in a dangerous state. A bit over the edge. You know

that, don't you, Roxie. And I think you know where
he is.'

'I said.' Her voice was gruff.

'You said a tunnel by the pier. I think you could be
much more precise if you wanted.'

He tapped the driver on the shoulder. 'Let's take a
drive around and you shall tell me when we get warm.
Like a child's game. Cold, warm, warmer, and hot.'
He motioned to Inspector Lane, who got in beside
him. There was already a woman detective in the car,
acting as driver.

Roxie drew herself into the corner as if she wanted
to get as far away from them as she could. 'I don't
want to see him.'

'You won't have to.'

'And I don't want him to see me.'

'I can't promise anything. But I'll do my best.'

'Come on now, Roxie,' said the sergeant from the
front seat. 'Tell me which way to go.' She was driving
efficiently towards Greenwich, just approaching the
park.

'You'll find him soon enough. I gave you what help
I could. Look underground, look near the pier, like I
said. By the *Cutty Sark*. And then look out.'

'What do you mean, Roxie?' Coffin took her up
sharply.

In a harsh voice, Roxie said, 'He's got a gun.'

'I see.' Coffin looked towards Paul Lane, who
shook his head. No, his men were not armed.

'There's worse than that.' Roxie paused. 'I think
he's got some explosive on him too.'

PETER AND NONA had their backs against a wall, they were facing the man who seemed to inhabit the tunnel. Live there did not seem to be quite the word for someone whose residence there appeared so transient. He had a sleeping-bag, a torch propped up on two slabs of stone, and a couple of carrier bags. An overnight case had been placed carefully on a sheet of newspaper.

He also had a gun.

Nona felt the wall pressing into her back. Peter reached out and took her hand. This wasn't going right. He was The Master, but no one would know it. This wasn't how it should be. Nona knew it too, he could see in her face.

'Let her go,' said the man. 'Move a step apart. I don't want you two to be close to each other.'

He was a short man, still clinging on to youth in his clothes and the cut of his hair. His pale grey suit and suede jacket were stylish, even if now creased and grubby. He had managed to shave somehow.

Peter did not move. The man waved the gun in his face. 'You don't know me, remember that. And you won't remember me when I'm away. I'm just a man. Call me that.'

'Do what he says,' whispered Nona, who was frightened. She knew that there were several personal matters about her that could arouse the man, and that it was better to be cautious. It was hateful to have to be like that, and usually she did not allow herself to think on those lines, but it was there and had to be recognized as a factor. Probably Peter did not see it.

Peter muttered something resentful under his breath, but did as she asked. Just one small pace. He was not particularly frightened himself, more excited and interested than alarmed, but he did not want to endanger Nona. He sensed already that her position was more vulnerable than his own. He could see it in the man's eyes and the manner in which his gaze lingered on Nona.

He could understand it. There was a lot about Nona that made her very vulnerable indeed, and which she seemed unaware of. In a way, this irked him and always had done. He felt she should know. Even while he admired Nona and loved her, there were times he wanted to say: 'Look, Nona, there is this thing you have to take into account between us.' But he had not yet mastered a way of putting it into words.

He reached out and took her hand. At this moment it was for him to protect her, and he must find a way to do it. Somehow the chap, who had plainly gone over the top, he could understand that, must be convinced they were no threat to him. He tried.

'We won't say anything. We'll say we only came exploring. Just let us out. It's nothing to do with us, you being here.' Be a troglodyte if you want to be, he thought. Stay as long as you like. Die here. See if I care. He did not let himself think how this man had killed Billy Egan, nor the ferocity he had shown. He could understand, even appreciate, the violence, but he did not want it turned against himself and Nona. Not that way.

'Sit down.'

Nona looked down at her clean jeans and pretty shirt, then she slid on to the floor, ignoring a patch of dirt. Reluctantly Peter sat down beside her.

'Don't touch,' said the man again. 'Keep well apart.'

Peter moved about an inch. The man, all right, call him 'the man', seemed satisfied. He moved back himself and leaned against the wall, studying them. He picked the stub of a half-smoked cigarette out of his pocket and lit it.

He smoked it deliberately in slow puffs, giving Peter time to consider their situation.

Their captor, if that was what he was, stood between them and the way out. They were probably strong enough if they acted as a team to push him aside, but he had the gun. If it was loaded.

Somehow, from the way he handled it, Peter thought it was loaded.

He bent down to stare at the floor. He could sense that the man was more afraid and taut than he was himself. He could pick up the fear. Smell it almost, although the man, a natty dresser by Peter's standards, had loaded himself with aftershave.

He tried again. 'If you let us out, we'll just walk away.'

The man dropped the tiny fraction of the cigarette that he could not smoke to the ground, letting the last acrid smoulder of it rise in the air. Nona coughed.

'Shut up. I'm thinking.'

Nona said, politely and carefully, 'I think you are being silly. You haven't harmed us. Let us go now and there will be no trouble for you. Why should there be?'

In defiance of the man, Peter reached out and took her hand, pressing it, trying to tell her to keep quiet. She was not showing her usual intelligence. 'The chap's not resting here,' Peter wanted to say to her, 'he's hiding. And if he's hiding, then he must have good reason for it.' But it was safer if Nona did not go on and dig this out of him. She might suspect the exact position; with her knowledge, she probably did, but much better not to say. There were rules, he willed her, follow them.

She spoke. 'Unless you are already in trouble.'

'I told you to shut up.'

For once Peter agreed with him. 'Don't go on, Nona.'

'We've been out a long while already. My parents will wonder where I am.'

If they're at home, thought Peter. 'It's only just after midday. We never had our picnic.'

'No.' She looked very white, and somehow surprised, as if her precious youth had never met such a threat before.

'Let's have it now.'

'I dropped the bag by the door.'

'I know you did.'

Of course he knew. He was sitting looking at it. But she was relaxing a little.

He reached out with his foot to drag the lunch bag towards him. Sarah would be surprised to know what had happened to her picnic.

'You can forget that,' said the man. 'Just sit still.'

Peter still quietly edged his right foot forward.

'Stay where you are.'

He drew back his foot. To his surprise, the man went over and kicked the bag towards him.

'Go on. Eat it if you like.'

Good thing or bad thing? Bad, probably. It meant they were here for some long time. When things went wrong in this kind of game, they went very wrong.

He pressed his back against the stone wall and stretched out his hand for some food. Nona shook her head before he had a chance to offer her anything. He knew that was the wrong way to be, she ought to try to eat. It was a gesture of strength to the man who held them prisoner, if nothing else. She was one of those who, in time of crisis, cannot eat. He himself could always eat; he would have made a good soldier. He bit into one of Sarah's ham and cucumber sandwiches; his taste buds appreciated them. He took another one. Although not given to dramatic expressions, he found himself thinking: End of Act One.

DOWN BY the *Cutty Sark,* the police search had begun again. Now they knew where they were going.

In an office on the pier Coffin and Lane had maps spread out in front of them. The room was full of policemen, as well as the Chief Superintendent and the Inspector, there was the officer in charge of the search and a sergeant. The woman detective had gone off with Roxie Farmer to give her a cup of tea and sit in her house keeping an eye on her.

'That's the tunnel.' Coffin pointed to a line on the map, running from the river to the park. It even had a name, he could just make out the tiny print. 'Victory Tunnel. Which victory would that be?'

'Trafalgar, I should think,' said the pier official. He was an elderly man who had worked on the river all his life and regarded his present job as something of a rest on the way to full retirement. But he loved the river which was his life. His name, Waters, befitted him. 'Or even the Armada. It's all old stuff round here.'

'Usable still, is it?'

'We keep everything in good order. But you won't get in it easily now that tide's up. Wait until it goes down and you can walk in without getting your feet wet.'

'Can't we approach by boat?'

'We'll do that anyway, but it's still better to have the tide with you.' He had a proper respect for the river as all must who work on her. He suspected Coffin of lacking it.

'I'd like to go now.'

It was an order.

THE ATMOSPHERE in the tunnel had deteriorated in the last two hours as the cigarette smoke had grown thicker.

Unless their captor had a secret supply of them, Peter reckoned he would be out of smokes before they moved.

They would be moving, and he pondered about that move, thinking about the gun. He had no idea what the time was. He did not have a watch, the only time-piece in the family was an aged alarm clock sitting on the kitchen shelf. Nona had a watch with a pretty red face, but she was sitting with her hands in her lap with the watch hidden. He knew better than to ask her the time; she was edgy enough as it was. So was Their Captor. That was his official title now in Peter's mind. That made him both easier to think about (for were there not rules about Captors? Rules of War) and infinitely more dangerous.

'Let her go,' he said suddenly and loudly, more loudly than he had meant. 'Let her get off and I'll stay.'

Nona raised her head and looked at Peter hopefully. 'I wouldn't leave you.'

He ignored this as valiant but untrue. She would certainly go if she got the chance, and he would not blame her.

'Let her go,' he repeated.

'We'll all move together, when we go,' said the man. He was sitting on the ground near his packages over which he kept a protective, hostile arm, as if he did not want anything of his touched. 'I'll go first, then you after me.'

'When?'

'When it's dark and the time is right. Do you think I've been staying here for the good of my health? I'm waiting for the tide.' It was the longest sentence he had said since they got there. There had been occasional mutterings to himself over his cigarettes, but nothing spoken to them. This was almost a conversation, and not a fuck or a shit in it. There had been quite a lot of those in the sentences directed at himself.

'Why can't we go first?'

'Because I say not.' And he looked at his gun. 'I have the right to say. And who gave me that Right.'

For the first time, Peter felt fear. And also a tremendous sense of excitement. This is it, he thought, this is how it should be, Power is crackling through me.

IRENE PITT HAD her lunch with Christopher, saw that he was deeply preoccupied with his election chances, not thinking about her at all, and wondered if she was going to enjoy being married to a politician.

'Oh, come on, now. There may not be a General Election.'

'Got to be,' he said gloomily. 'He'll have to go. If not now, then soon.'

'He wouldn't dare do it.'

'Things happen. He's not a lucky PM. He's got trouble.' Nothing like President Carter's, of course, but sufficient.

No, it really was not going to be much fun being married to a politician. Then she caught Chris's eyes, and yes, it was, after all. You could change your mind three times in as many seconds, and that was the exhausting thing about being in love. Age didn't seem to make any difference.

After their lunch (so called, but not much was eaten), she went shopping, met a friend to discuss future work plans and finally went home.

Edward appeared at the door of his study as soon as he heard her key in the door.

'Where's Nona?'

'Out. She was going on a picnic.'

'It's time she was back.'

'It's not late.' She looked at the wall clock. It was a household with a number of clocks, all of them accurate.

'Late enough.'

'Oh, come on.'

Edward said angrily: 'The sooner this divorce is over and done with, the better.'

'Eddy, why are you like this suddenly. You never were in New York. You were happy enough about it. After all, you had always got...' She did not utter what he had always got. But he had always had Someone.

'I wish we had never come back to this house.'

It might, indeed, have been better.

THE RIVER POLICE provided a boat, an escort and much expert advice. They showed signs of wanting to take the whole operation over, but Coffin, backed up by his Inspector, would have none of it.

They piled into the motor launch.

'We will make a fair noise, let him know we are coming,' commented Lane. 'Wouldn't it be better to sneak up quietly? By rowing.'

'No. I don't mind if he hears us coming. See what he does.'

'We can shout if you like,' said the man piloting the launch agreeably.

'No. No voices. Just the sound of the launch's engine.'

'Right you are.'

They chugged down river from the pier towards the entrance to the tunnel. The tide, as predicted, covered the little path by which Peter and Nona had arrived, and lapped at the wooden door.

A plastic bag floated in the water.

'Someone round here shops at Harrods,' said Coffin. 'And I don't think it's Terry Place.'

He fished out the bag to examine it. 'Had chocolates in it. There's still one in it, stuck to the bottom. Looks quite fresh.' He added, thoughtfully, 'Wonder if there's anyone inside with him?'

That made a difference.

THEY HEARD the engine of the motor launch inside the tunnel. It was clearly audible in the silence. No one had said anything for a long time.

'I can hear an engine.' Nona scrambled to her feet. She opened her mouth to shout. Terry Place clamped his hand over her mouth, stifling her cries.

'Shut up, you bitch.'

Nona bit his hand in a fury of frustration and fear. He hit at her face with the gun, but she jerked her head back. Peter lunged forward to protect Nona, but the gun was stuck in Nona's neck.

'Please,' whispered Nona, her eyes on Peter.

'Move another inch and she'll have it.'

'That won't do you any good if it's escape you're looking for.' But Peter drew back.

'I'll kill myself before I let myself be taken in.'

'You won't kill yourself,' said Peter. 'I know you. You mind how you look. I've seen a dead man, a man who killed himself, and he looked terrible. He soiled his clothes so he stank, and his face was all swollen and black. You wouldn't like to look like that.'

'Don't,' said Nona.

OUTSIDE in the launch a conference was going on.

'Like to know who's in there with him.' Coffin was still holding the bag which had held chocolates. 'Some wretched tourists, I suppose. Wonder how they got there?'

'Same way as he did,' said the river policeman. 'You can walk when the tide's right. If he's there, of course.'

'I think he is.' Roxie had thought so, and Coffin believed she understood her brother. Didn't like him, feared him even, but knew the way his mind worked. 'We're sure there's no way out the other end?'

'There was once,' said Lane. 'According to the map. Came out just by the Old Observatory. Near the Meridian. But the chap in the office says a bomb went down there in the war and there was a landfall. The tunnel is blocked. He was clear on that. You heard him.'

'He's caught like a rat in a trap, then.'

They stayed quietly in the launch, waiting and listening. Everything was still.

At home, in Church Row, Nona's parents were just beginning to get worried about her. Sarah had hardly thought about her brother yet, but she did wonder when he missed his tea. No Fleming ever missed his tea, it was the main meal of the day, and Sarah was very good at producing tasty dishes like Toad in the Hole and homemade deep apple pie. She was an enterprising cook, as she was in all things, and fed her family well.

All the same, she was surprised when Edward and Irene Pitt turned up on her doorstep.

'No,' she said. 'I don't know where they are. Just out. They are grown up, you know. I didn't expect Pete home any special time.' Privately, she thought that Irene and Edward must be living in the past. You didn't expect people to clock in these days.

But in the end she agreed to go with the Pitts to the local police station to express concern about the absentees. She refused to regard them as missing. It meant taking Weenie and Co., who had to be made tidy and neat, so it was some time before their caravan set forth.

Weenie and the others piled into Edward's car with relish. An outing. What luck. One had to hope, Sarah thought, that they wouldn't be sick.

On the river, another police launch had arrived to complement the first one. They were in radio contact with their base.

'He's in there,' said Coffin. He had decided to make a move. 'Let's give him a shout.'

'Terry! Terry Place, we know it's you. Open up and come out.'

The noise echoed over the water which seemed to suck up the sound. They tried again. You didn't expect an answer straight away.

Suddenly, from inside the tunnel, they heard first a shot and then a scream. There was no mistaking the sex of the screamer.

'Who's the girl?' said Coffin.

FOR ONCE communication of information was brisk and free, all channels seemed to be open and listening to each other.

Another launch from the river police arrived to help keep watch on the mouth of the tunnel. More policemen took up station on the river walk. A cordon was thrown round the area. For the moment they were sitting and waiting.

From the local police came the story of the missing girl and boy. As soon as he heard the story, John Coffin had himself taken back to the police centre dealing with the case. The Pitts were glad to see someone they knew.

Irene Pitt was shown the plastic bag which had once contained chocolates. She identified it at once.

White and anxious, she said: Yes, she had given that bag to her daughter, and it had contained such chocolates.

The young policeman from Bromley reported that he had seen a young couple whose description matched the wanted pair and they had gone towards the pier. 'I watched because they were a striking couple. He had red hair and she was beautiful. Very striking. They went down a flight of steps on the river walk. No, I didn't see any more. Couldn't from where I was. They were out of view.'

Sarah Fleming answered the few questions that came her way with concise intelligence. John Coffin questioned her himself. Yes, it sounded like Peter. He did have red hair and he had certainly been interested in the whole area down by the river walk. It was something of an obsession with him. No, she didn't know Terry Place and she would be surprised if Peter did. He only liked people of his own generation.

Bright kid, Coffin thought. What's she keeping back? He sensed there was something. 'We'll arrange a car home for you and that lot,' he said, giving her a smile and Weenie (who was stamping on his foot) a severe look. 'Try not to worry.'

She was surprised how unhappy and anxious she felt. It was almost a pleasure to deal with a tantrum from Weenie, and a positive relief to be sent home in a police car. She knew that the Pitts were going to stay with the police, go down to the river to wait if the Chief Superintendent let them, but she did not want to. You had to trust Peter. She did trust Peter.

'Now we know who is in there with Place. He's got the girl, Nona, and the lad. The girl is frightened but alive. About the boy we don't know.'

'We heard a shot,' said Lane. 'He could be hurt. Or even dead.'

'That's looking on the black side.'

'We can get bugs fastened to the door. They'll pick up anything inside. That way we will know who is in there and where.'

'And how long to get them fixed?'

The man shrugged. 'Depends.'

Coffin looked across the water. 'I don't think we've got much time.'

Inside the tunnel, Peter said to Terry Place: 'That wasn't very clever, what you did just now, firing the gun. Now they know you're inside.'

'They knew that anyway.'

'You could have kept them guessing.' Peter felt immensely stronger than Place, and in charge.

'And now they know you are frightened as well.'

After a period of silence from outside, a voice now hailed Place, told him to come out and give himself up.

By some freak of the acoustics his name seemed to echo round and round the chamber. Place, Place, Place.

The three of them had come back down the tunnel to the entrance, with the man pushing Nona in front of him as a hostage.

Nona whispered to Peter: 'What's going to happen.'

'I don't know.'

From the river the disembodied voice said: 'Let the girl go. Send her out.'

Place took no action, but the other two could see he was listening.

The voice started again: 'Send her out before we come in, and we won't hurt you.'

'Why don't you do it?' Peter had the question ready. 'It would be better.'

Once again the voice outside spoke: 'Open up, Place.'

'Let her go,' said Peter, 'and I'll stay. You've still got me.'

'No.' Place moved forward quickly. He grabbed Nona by the waist, held her against him, with the gun pressed to her neck. 'She stays, you go.'

'I won't.' Give in to this man and you're lost, Peter thought. He's mad, gone over the top.

'Get on with it.'

Nona looked at Peter with fear in her eyes. 'Please. Do what he says.'

Slowly Peter opened the door to the river and stood there at the opening, the water lapping at his feet.

Behind him Place and Nona shuffled into place so that all three were visible to the police on the river.

Coffin stood up in the launch facing them. 'So that's how it is? You're a fool, Place. And your own worst enemy. Let the kid go.'

A small fleet of boats were now in position in an arc around the entrance. Place could not see the police presence on the river walk above his head, but he could probably guess it was there.

He shouted out his demands. A car to get away with. No pursuit. No helicopter to hang overhead. If they let this happen he would shoot the girl. Otherwise he would release her when he felt safe.

Peter did not believe this for a moment. Nona would not go free. She would be shot. It was up to him to save her and he knew how to do it.

He was standing directly in front of Terry Place, with Nona to his right. He measured the distance between his foot and Place's leg, then between Nona and the river's edge. The tide was already on the turn, you could just see the stone margin of the path they had walked.

I am a horse, he told himself. A great horse with powerful hooves. He delivered a great kick backwards at Terry Place's shins, the edge of his boots like iron.

As Place screamed and stumbled, Peter grabbed Nona. 'Jump! Jump into the river!'

Behind him he heard Place scrambling, then there was a shot. Did it come from behind or from the water? Then a flurry of shots.

And as he and Nona hit the water, the world exploded into light and fire.

FIVE

IT WAS A ROOM with a lot of clocks. John Coffin thought he had never sat in a room with so many clocks. One on a table, one on a desk, and a third on the wall. Watches as well, everyone in the room was wearing a watch. Time had never been so well watched over.

He felt intimidated, and perhaps was meant to feel so. He was sitting facing the Assistant Commissioner (Crime), across a desk so neat and orderly and so well polished that you knew no serious work could be done at it. In fact, the AC had another and smaller office which he really used. This one was for show, to see people, to hold the sort of meeting he was holding now.

A kind of court, Coffin thought sourly.

It was an unofficial meeting with official overtones. The unofficial side was represented by the friendly way he was being offered coffee in a thin china cup, and the official side by the nervous energy of the AC's manner and the fact that he was unobtrusively taking notes.

Coffin was almost glad to taste that the coffee was as mediocre as always. It made him feel more at home.

He looked back on the last ten days, reflecting on the events which had brought him to where he now was.

Ten days ago a police bullet had hit the explosive which Terry Place had hidden in a carrier bag in the tunnel. It was about six feet from him when it went off, to which distance, and the fact that Peter's kick had made him roll into the water at the minute of explosion, he owed his mangled survival. What had come through was not quite a complete Terry Place, but one substantially still himself. He remained in the intensive care unit of the local hospital and under police guard.

The youngsters, Peter and Nona, had been hurt by blast and Peter had been burnt in the back, but they had come off lightly. The river Thames had received them with some kindness, not passing on to them hepatitis or typhoid or any of the other plagues its waters might be carrying. They had had hospital treatment but were now at home.

One policeman had suffered a detached retina from the blast and one onlooker had had a heart attack. Several more had complained of shock.

Coffin himself had injured his back helping the girl and boy out of the water. His own fault, he should have left it to the river police who had more experience of that sort of thing, but he had felt responsible. Which brought him to why he was here.

'Who gave the order to fire?' asked the AC.

'I did.'

'You had information that Place was armed?'

'Yes. I had what seemed reliable information that Place had both a gun and explosive.' Roxie had been dead right too, as it turned out. 'He was a man with a record of violence. So I asked for guns to be issued, and that was done.'

'And who fired first?'

'Place did,' said Coffin firmly.

'And all necessary warnings were given.'

'Yes.' Yes, bloody yes, Coffin said inside himself.

But a journalist on a local paper had claimed that the police had fired the first shot and without shouting a warning to Place. He had got his story into the national press. Once that happened an inquiry hung over Coffin's head.

Without warning, he had fallen into just the sort of trouble he ought to have kept out of. He knew how unloved he and the TAS unit were locally. Bernard Jones had told him, even if he hadn't known. No tears were going to be shed for him.

There was something very handy about the way this story had come out. At the moment he couldn't say more than that, but he was thinking about it. It would be paranoia, of course, to suggest that someone had arranged for him to drop into this particular hole, but it was certainly true that no one would be eager to fish him out. Not locally, anyway.

'A witness has come forward to say he heard the police fire before Place. Two shots from one direction.'

'Not true,' said Coffin bluntly. 'The witness is mistaken.'

So there they were with two conflicting stories. One of the clocks struck the hour, then significantly after it, a second chimed. The third clock remained silent, but as if to compensate, a watch on the AC's wrist gave a tiny chirp.

The thing that annoyed him most was that this was all such a waste of time when there was work to do. The murder of William Egan for a start. Terence Place, although highly favoured for the job, had not confessed and might never do so. He might die before he had a chance to speak at all.

And apart from this one case there were several others lining up for his attention. Not to mention an urgent telephone call from Laetitia about a trip to Glasgow.

Coffin drank his cold sweet coffee down to the bottom of the cup.

'ALL THE FORENSIC evidence ties Place to the murder of Bill Egan. He had the motive and opportunity. His own behaviour bears out his guilt, but there are still one or two questions I would like answered.' Coffin was speaking almost to himself. It was the end of the day that had started with the interview in the dark-panelled room with the clocks.

Coffin and Inspector Paul Lane were talking privately over a drink in the Victory Arms, a pub whose windows gave them a view of the sails of the *Cutty Sark*. Something was needed to take away the taste of the coffee and the interview with the AC. Lane, who knew of the session, had carefully not mentioned it.

Across the room, also having a drink, were the two young sergeants who were the rest of the TAS unit. They were showing loyalty to their boss by drinking there. They were a team.

Coffin looked around. 'Where's Jumbo?' Jumbo was the nickname of the large chief inspector, Jimmy Jardine, who was his direct assistant.

'Gone home,' said Paul Lane. Jumbo was not happy working with them and they all knew it. He was even less happy now, and anyway preferred his garden and a glass of wine to beer and the Victory Arms.

Coffin accepted the information without comment. 'I wish I knew a bit more about Place.'

'Don't we all?'

They knew all about his birth, upbringing, schooling and police record, but something essential was missing.

Paul Lane was occupied in putting together the formal structure of the police case against Terence Place which would then go to the DPP. As he said himself, with something of a mixed metaphor: 'The baby seemed to have all its parts but was liable to fall to pieces in the hand.'

He was more irritated than Coffin by what he felt was the untidiness of the case. He was a man who liked his cases to be neat, to be finished in broad brush strokes. Now he was getting a lesson in the complexities of human relationships. Coffin had been at it long enough to know that was the way truth lay, that in the untidiness lay the answers. If he was honest he would admit that the shifting surface, the muddy underside fascinated him. What he looked for, really.

'Yes, we need Place's testimony.'

'But you believe he did kill Egan?'

'Oh, sure of it. We've got the right man. But there are some worries.'

'I feel the same way.'

'To begin with, where was Egan all the time before he was killed? We still don't know. Not for sure. We've made a guess from the piece of paper found in the pocket of Place's coat.' Was he hiding in No. 22? And if so, how?

'I'd like to know why Place murdered his father-in-law so savagely,' said Lane. 'Kill him, yes, but to do it that particularly brutal way puzzles me. He never was a nice man, but he wasn't a sadist.'

'I think I can explain that: he was frightened.'

But that only posed another question: Why so frightened?

'Do you know,' Coffin went on, 'I think there is a third figure in this case. One we haven't focused on yet.'

'Roxie Farmer?'

'Could be.'

'Or the wife?'

'More likely. Where is she, by the way?'

'In her own flat. She flew home from Spain yesterday.'

'She didn't hurry.'

'No, not much love lost there. She would have preferred Terry to die quickly, but as long as he dies, I reckon she'll be easy.'

'What about her father?'

Lane shrugged. 'Hard to know.'

'I'll have to see her.'

'You won't enjoy the meeting. She's her father's daughter. Got a tongue on her.'

The two young sergeants watched their senior depart.

'Guvnor's in a bad mood.' The speaker was an ambitious young graduate, seeking accelerated promotion and not pleased at the notion he might have got into an accident-prone unit. But David Evans was a fair-minded young man, and knew from his historical studies that bad luck cannot be avoided by even the greatest of men. Look at Julius Caesar, Abraham Lincoln and John F. Kennedy. Still, he did not propose to offer his own career for assassination. 'Can't blame him,' he said tolerantly. 'I shall look out for a move.'

His partner was both less well educated and a sharper observer of his boss. 'I shouldn't, if I were you. Never looks good going out on a falling tide. And I've seen the old man in this state before. He always gets up.' He might have added: But he has a long memory for those that let him down.

JOHN COFFIN WALKED down Church Row on his way home, cutting through Queen Charlotte's Alley, on purpose to have a look at the house where the Flem-

ings lived. All looked in order, but there had been no
laundry done for him lately. Couldn't blame the girl,
but he was running a bit short. It was amazing how his
underwear and the case seemed to be involved in a
kind of dance, in which the arrival home of his shirts
might depend on who was found guilty of what.

He considered calling, he knew Peter was back from
the hospital, but decided to put the visit off until
morning. Weenie and Co. might be at school then and
he wanted a word with Sarah on her own.

One of the Flemings' neighbours was outside, pol-
ishing his car, a nice-looking Audi.

Sign of the times, he thought, as he turned the corner into Church Row. He could remember when a
barrow, or a donkey and cart, would have been the
mark of riches in the Alley and not an imported Ger-
man car. He had known this district all his life, had
come back to it as a young police detective for his first
major case, and its vitality and capacity for change
amazed him.

Under his arm, neatly wrapped in white paper (once
it would have been newsprint, yesterday's evening paper), he had his supper. Fish and chips, the Londoner's favourite take-away meal. The fish shop had a
rival now in Padovani's Pizza Parlour next door. The
Padovani family had long been known to John Coffin since they had once run a restaurant near where he
had lodged as a young detective. Now they had a
smart restaurant in Blackheath, another in Knights-
bridge, and a chain of pizza houses. Londoners for
four generations, they went back triumphantly each

year to the village in Italy from which they had sprung to buy wine and show off their wealth. And occasionally to bring back a bride.

He could see down the road to No. 22. The Pitts had certainly livened up the appearance of their house since their return. The window-boxes were in full bloom. But there was a FOR SALE board up, new today, he hadn't seen it there this morning when he set out for the meeting with the AC.

Mrs Brocklebank had been quiet lately about the tragic possibilities of the house, but he did not think she had forgotten. By no means. He had seen a thoughtful look in her eyes. Could you have with a bad character, an actively hostile house?

Of course you couldn't. He was a rational man and a police officer, but No. 22 seemed obstinately to be producing its own evidence. He studied the front of the house. Just an ordinary house. Might have a word with Mrs Brocklebank, he thought, just as the front door of No. 22 opened.

Irene Pitt came out of her house and saw him.

He walked forward. 'Good evening. How's Nona?'

Irene hesitated. 'Pretty well recovered. Almost herself again.' Irene looked less sleekly groomed than usual. Her hair was untidy and her lipstick chewed away.

'It was a bad experience for her.' How bad he was in a good position to know, he saw that in Irene's eyes. Judgement as well; he couldn't blame her.

'I think she still has the odd nightmare. We're sending her away.' Irene's gaze moved to the FOR SALE board.

'I'm sorry you're going.'

'Yes. Well, that might have happened anyway. Probably would have done. I don't think Edward would have wanted to stay on, and I was leaving. This just hurried things along.'

Aware of his supper rapidly cooling under his arm, Coffin nevertheless let the conversation go on. If Irene wanted to talk, then she should.

'We're grateful to the boy for saving Nona's life.'

'Yes, he probably did that,' Coffin agreed gravely.

'But then he got her into the trouble in the first place. Still, I blame myself too. So I'm staying home, trying to be a good mother and cooking all their favourite meals.' She noticed the bundle under his arm. 'Fish and chips? I'm off there myself. It's what Edward likes best. Tomorrow or the next day, it will be curry soup and lasagne, that's for Nona.'

'Invite me round.'

'So I will. But I have to make my own curry powder, the bought stuff won't do.'

'There's a spice stall in Greenwich market.' He had seen it there.

'I'll take a look.' Then she said suddenly: 'I want to get out of here. The house, the street, the district. I don't think it's good for us. I don't know where is, but here is wrong. I don't think people hate us personally, but we don't fit in.'

He did not dispute this, but he was troubled. 'It was not the cause of what happened to Nona.'

'No? But it's part of it.'

She had said to him what she had wanted to say and now she was off. 'I thought you'd understand.'

Coffin nodded. He did understand.

'Give my love to your sister.'

'I will.' He understood the need for her to say that, too. The message was the message.

ON THE NEXT DAY he took Lane with him, together with a woman detective whose services he had borrowed, and went round the corner into Queen Charlotte's Alley to visit Sarah Fleming. There was no need really for such a high-powered delegation. He could have sent one detective-sergeant from his unit, but he felt personal about this.

He went breakfastless, his fish and chip supper still rumbling uneasily around inside him. He had left Mrs Brocklebank cleaning his flat, and she did not look herself either.

She said as much. 'I'm not myself this morning. Brock said to me, "Old girl, you need a rest," and I said, "Brock, I shall take one." So after today, I shall not be cleaning you for a week.'

'Once the Pitts have sold up, you won't have to clean there.' Might not be a very cheering remark for her, as he thought she liked her employers. Good payers too, or he misjudged them.

'Someone will always need to clean up that house,' she had responded gloomily and ambiguously.

Sarah Fleming saw them coming through the window of the front room. It was her practice to watch Weenie and Co. off to school, but without letting them know she did it. She had trained them to hold hands, walk straight to school and not to talk to strangers. Sometimes she thought that when they were old enough to be doubtful strangers themselves she would still be telling them to hold hands and watch the traffic.

Peter was lying on the sofa in the room behind. It was an old sofa, but had been a good one in its day, made of soft leather which had worn to a comfortable softness.

'We've got visitors.'

'Oh.' It was a listless sound. Peter lay back on the cushions. Officially he had recovered nicely from the shock of his experience, but his sister thought he needed more time: she was mothering him.

She let her mind run over the events of yesterday. Peter had come back from hospital on his own but in tearing good spirits. 'I rescued her,' he said. 'I saved Nona. I did. Nothing can take that away. We shall see each other soon.' He looked rapt.

Edward Pitt had called on them in the evening. He had come in and asked to see Peter. Then he took his hand, and thanked him. Peter said very little but the glow was still on him.

'I want you to know how grateful to you we are. We can't repay you for what you've done. Never. But this represents our effort to try.' He handed an envelope over to Peter. 'Might help with your training for whatever. Or buy a car.'

'Nona . . .' began Peter.

'We're sending her to New York to stay with friends. Seems best. She sends love.'

There was a bit more talk, more thanks, and then he was gone.

'He paid me,' said Peter. 'He paid me off.'

Sarah had said nothing. Nothing to say. She had concentrated on keeping him warm and preparing the food he liked best. It always worked with Weenie when she had a misery. They all had miseries, it was one of the things in their family. Sudden great glooms of engulfing horribleness. But they came out of them, as a rule, in no time at all.

'The visitors are the police.'

Peter shrugged. 'Don't want to see them.'

'Chief Inspector John Coffin.'

'Oh, you call him that, do you?'

'And two others. They mean business.'

She recognized the woman. She had called on them when their parents died. Peter might know her too.

Buried in their past, like a rock in a desert, was the death of their parents. They never spoke of it. Still, it was there, and occasionally you walked on it and banged your foot. She thought it could no longer draw blood, the time for that was past.

Without waiting for the ring, she opened the door and let them in. 'Good morning, Chief Inspector.' She smiled nervously at Sergeant Phyllis Henley, who had been kind to her at the time of their parents' ungainly departure from life, but uncompromising. The only one she did not know was Inspector Lane. No one introduced him, but she found out his name later from a newspaper.

They crowded in, all rather large people. As she looked at them squashing themselves into chairs bought for Weenie and Co., she thought of the story from her French course. Madame de Sévigné telling the story of the poisoner, Madame de Brinvilliers, about to undergo the water torture. Looking up at the great leather bag of water and the funnel to be inserted into her mouth, the murderess had said, 'What, all that water for poor little me?'

All those policemen for poor little them?

Sergeant Henley said, as if it was all her show, which it could not have been: 'How are things with you, Sarah?'

'Very well.' Sarah knew she sounded prim. 'I'm managing beautifully.'

'Yes, you are.' Could that be admiration in the tough lady's voice? Respect, anyway. Sarah was almost shocked. 'But what about the others?'

'They're doing all right.'

As if she had had a signal from the Chief Inspector, Sergeant Henley subsided and Coffin took over the questioning. Because it soon became apparent to Sarah, if not Peter, that this was what it was.

He took the boy through the whole episode. Very quietly and not pressing too much on details at first, getting him talking. Then: What was the purpose of this walk. Why had they gone?

'We were just out for a picnic and bit of sightsee-ing. The *Cutty Sark* and all that.'

'Why did you look in the tunnel?'

Peter just gave a shrug. 'Just taking a look.'

'It must have been a shock to you to find Terry Place there?'

Peter nodded.

'You didn't know him?'

Peter shook his head.

Sarah got up. 'I'll make some coffee. Or a cup of tea?'

Coffin said quietly: 'Stay where you are, Sarah.' He thought: I'll get her on her own and have a private talk. He knew more now about the family, and how they had lost their parents. He had a lot of sympathy for the girl, she had taken on a lot and was doing it well. Keeping her own identity together too. Some girls would have been completely submerged. He smiled at her. 'Coffee later, eh?'

Turning again to Peter, he said: 'Let's talk about the shooting. Did you jump before Place shot at you or after?'

Peter thought about it. 'All seemed to happen at once.'

And that was the trouble, Coffin thought. It prob-ably had. He tried again. 'Think about it. What made you jump at that moment? Was it the sound of a shot?'

'No. I'd made up my mind there was a chance for us.'

'So probably Place shot at you in reaction?' And that would make his shot the first.

Peter shrugged. 'Could be.'

Coffin saw that it was as far as they were going to get now. Nona Pitt next, he thought.

'We'll have that coffee now, Sarah,' he said. 'If the offer still holds.'

They would talk to Nona Pitt next.

As they left, Phyllis Henley said: 'Makes a good cup of coffee, that girl.' In a quiet way she was a heavy drinker and often needed a dash of caffeine in the morning.

'Does everything well, I should think.' It was Paul Lane's first contribution. 'Nice kid.'

'Seen the others?' asked the Sergeant. 'I never know what to make of them, but they certainly make you think about the future of the human race.'

She was not an optimistic woman.

They walked back down Queen Charlotte's Alley towards Church Row and No. 22. But the Pitts were denied them. No one answered the door.

'Out.' Coffin turned away after his third ring on the bell. There were plenty of other tasks for all three to get on with, and he might not bring Phyllis Henley tomorrow, he would prefer a more conciliatory personality, although she certainly knew her district. He thought he had it pretty clear from Peter's testimony that Place had indeed fired first and that the boy knew it. Nona might be able to confirm this for them. 'I'll see them tomorrow.'

And he did.

MRS BROCKLEBANK WAS the first into No. 22 Church Row next day and the first to see the Pitts.

All of them, all except the boy, who as a weekly boarder at his school was never at home midweek.

She picked up the milk bottle, muttering to herself about how bad her back was and about her deep inner conviction that the steps would need scrubbing again. She couldn't see the stain; owing to the rain it was all dark, but of course it was there.

She went straight down to the kitchen in the basement where her mutterings turned into a clear expression of disgust at the mess, cooking vessels all over the place and nothing cleared up.

She climbed back up the stairs to the dining-room. She opened the door.

For a second she stood quite still, unable to believe what she was seeing. She took one step forward, then realized she could not go on. There was something wrong with her legs. She groped her way to the front door.

Stumbling, dizzy, she fumbled her way to No. 5 where she lay on the bell.

Coffin was shaving while drinking a mug of coffee. Morning was never his best time. Damn the bell! Ignore it. No, impossible to ignore it. On and on ringing. Someone must be lying on it.

A minute later, and he was running down the street, shaving and coffee unfinished.

Into No. 22, the front door left open wide by Mrs Brocklebank in her flight, then to the dining-room.

'My God.'

They were all three at the table where they had been sitting at a meal, the curry soup before them, a dreadful attic group, posed as for a stage set.

Edward had fallen forward, Irene had sagged towards the floor, and Nona still sat there, upright, supported by the arm of the chair.

But dead. They were all dead.

SIX

HE HAD KNOWN that the death of William Egan would not be the only death. He had even called it 'not the right death'. But to have this confirmation was hideous.

After they had been photographed, after the scene of crime team had swarmed in and over them, after the police surgeon and then a pathologist had done all that had to be done in that room, the bodies still stayed where they were.

Of much of this process Coffin was a spectator; he was unable to tear himself away. He had other tasks he could profitably have got on with, but he felt the need to stay. His mood was a mixture of incredulity and sadness. It was unbelievable what he saw and yet there it was. The scene of crime officer kept looking at him, as if he found him in the way but did not know how to say so.

The quiet and terrible peace of the death scene had been broken into by the need to measure, to check for fingerprints, and to find forensic debris. All over the room a search had gone on for what the scientists called 'forensic residues'. Disorder as well as death had now visited the room.

Coffin stayed until the bodies were packaged up and taken away to the police mortuary for the pathologist's investigation. He knew the pathologist, a woman doctor who had once been young but found her work was ageing her fast. Then he had a word with the scene of crime officer before he went away.

'Poison, of course.' He had sent Mrs Brocklebank home in a police car, and the headmaster of the boy's school had taken charge of the boy. Now he spoke almost to himself, but the other man answered.

'Looks like it, sir.' The young policeman was polite. 'But of course we'll know more when Professor Bearden has had a look.' He was businesslike and unmoved. This was certainly a strange case, but he had not known the Pitts and he saw plenty of messy deaths.

There was no sign of violence on the bodies, no bullet wounds, no stabbing, but signs of sudden convulsive death.

Edward Pitt had risen to his feet, knocking over his chair before collapsing. Irene had fallen across the table. Nona rested in her chair with her head back. He could see her open eyes. All three of them were still, with darkened faces as if the blood had been drawn upwards to the skin by capillary action, and there oxidized.

'I could almost name the poison,' said Coffin. 'But how? And why?'

Most of all why? Who could want to poison a whole family?

'There doesn't have to be a reason,' said the other man.

'You mean it's an accident?'

'No, sir. I meant sometimes there isn't a real reason. Not what you and I call a reason.' He shrugged. 'Maybe someone just didn't like the colour of their hair.'

You had to admit the truth of that, Coffin thought. But you didn't have to like it. Also, he was not going to accept it, he was going to look for a real motive for this murder. If it was murder and not some terrible accident.

He went off down the street, stepping lightly over the famous steps, which, without Mrs Brocklebank to clean them, looked sticky and stained. At some time something had certainly fallen on the steps, staining them for ever.

Coffin did not notice them. He believed in a lot of things, like natural justice, good money driving out bad, and the inequality of the sexes, but not in long-life blood.

COFFIN WENT BACK to his office, where the death of William Egan at the hands, as they believed, of his son-in-law Terry Place, was still being investigated. The latest report on Place's condition was that he would certainly live, and they might be able to speak to him tomorrow.

Meanwhile their investigation had received help from Roxie Farmer's reluctant admission that her brother had been staying with her, and that he had gone off one day, borrowing her former husband's bike, and had come back with blood on him. At the moment she could not remember which day this was, but she might be able to if she thought about it. And yes, she had recently lost a kitchen knife. For Roxie she had said a lot.

She had delivered herself of this statement to Inspector Paul Lane, who was gently triumphant at what he had got.

'She's delighted we've got Place and that he's really banged up. If he dies, she'll put on mourning but she won't cry.'

Coffin read her statement, and thought there were still questions to ask, such as, Was your brother on drugs and if so where did he get them? Or: Can you think of any other reason why he should kill with such a frenzy of violence? But meanwhile he must go to see Terence Place's wife, who also was not weeping.

Someone would have to tell Christopher Court, MP, that the woman he was expecting to marry was dead. Perhaps someone had done so already. And he himself would telephone Laetitia to tell her. Irene had been her friend. Have to do it gently, he told himself, no shocks for that pregnant lady. He thought with pleasure of his sister's elegant face with the skin that always had gleam and yet was softly, darkly creamy at the same time. Half-brother, half-sister, with Letty the child of his mother and a wartime alliance with a GI, they did not look alike.

He stared out of his office window where, instead of seeing the busy main road with buses and lorries running along it, another strong image filled his mind. Now he was looking at a building, possibly a house. In the middle, humping up the roof like an ungainly pillar, stood the death of William Egan at the hands of Terry Place; at one end, like a bearing wall, was the whole dead Pitt family, and then at the other end there sprouted, surprisingly, as a kind of ante chapel, the death of the student, Malcolm Kincaid. One of the three students who had appeared to be missing, and then had turned up. Malcolm was the one who had died later. By poison, just like the Pitts.

He was building this house and he did not know why.

He stretched out his hand to the telephone. Letty first, then Mrs Place. Out of one case, then into another. Or was it?

OTHER HOUSES, real houses, in the neighbourhood were being touched by what had happened to the Pitt family in No. 22, Church Row.

Sarah Fleming came home from her day at the Poly where she had heard the news of the killing in the college refectory. It was her habit after the lecture on the theory of economics, which she found particularly intractable as a subject, to take her notes (she was a sparse but efficient notetaker) to a quiet table by the window, drink some coffee and study what she had written down. If she understood it then, all was well. If not, there was still time to ask someone, or do some reading in the library. If she let the subject go cold on her, then she never got it straight in her mind. She knew her own areas of brilliance, she was a political philosopher and would make her mark in that subject if given time.

The refectory had been built when there was money around for building and the architect had let himself go with walls of glass and a high curving ceiling panelled in pastel colours. He had got a prize for the design, although the users of it would not now have endorsed this since it was both hot and noisy. It was known as 'the goldfish bowl'.

Sarah carried her cup of coffee and cheese roll back to her chosen table and settled to work. On days like this she resolutely closed her mind to worries about Weenie and Co., put thoughts about Peter aside, and concentrated on herself. It was the only way forward. She bit into her cheese roll. She would have preferred ham, being a natural meat-eater, but cheese was cheaper and money was always short with her. Fortunately the wedge of cheese was thick and tasty and for this she was grateful. She would have eaten it anyway because she was hungry, she was nearly always hungry, it was almost the only thing she had in common with Weenie.

A bit of roll, a drink of coffee, three pages of her text mastered. She was happy.

Unsurprised, she felt her happiness broken into.

'Sal?'

She looked up. Henrietta Fullove and Martin Jones. He had a father who was a police sergeant and always knew everything first. But to show he was independent and a big boy he had lately taken to spelling his name with a small letter: martin.

'You live in Greenwich, don't you? In Church Row?'

'Not Church Row. Just round the corner.'

'Not far, then. Did you know about the family that has been found dead? All of them. All in one room.'

Sarah stared in silence. Then she said: 'Who? What name?'

'Pitt.'

Sarah did not say: This is my own private area, this day, it is all I have, leave me alone. She accepted the invasion as she accepted everything that hit her, without hostility but with a strong inner resolve to fight back.

'Sit down, Martin.' She never knew how to make it come out sounding as if she was spelling it with a little 'm'. 'Hetty?'

'I'm off,' said Henrietta. 'Got a seminar. It's martin who wants to talk.' Miraculously, she could make it sound like a tiny tiny 'm'. But then she was planning to go on the stage and was already reputed to be collecting points for the Equity card.

Martin sat down; he had been wanting to get to know Sarah better for some time and this seemed like a good opportunity. 'The Pitts. Did you know them?'

'I knew them.' Although the episode with Terry Place and Nona and Peter had received publicity she had managed to conceal her connection with them. But of course she ought to have known that martin Jones would find out in the end. Obviously he did know from the look on his face. It was a nice face and, other things being equal, she would have responded to that first, she had been wanting to get to know him for a long time. 'Did you say all dead?'

'Yeah. Mass suicide perhaps. Or some accident. Murder even.'

'Is it in the papers yet? Or TV or radio?'

'No. But it will be.'

She didn't say: I must get home to Peter, but it was her thought. She still sat there. Peter did not read the newspapers, nor listen to the radio or watch television much; he read books or played his games. He wouldn't know yet, wouldn't know about Nona till she told him. She didn't want to be the one to do that although she knew it was her duty. Usually she did her duty.

She took a deep breath. Could she sit through their evening meal, knowing, and not telling? Yes. It might be best. So let someone else do it. A feeling of relief suffused her, a little of the burden she had assumed rolled off her shoulders.

'What's Church Row like?'

'It's a nice street.' That was true, anyway, but it was a lot of other things as well. The home of Nona Pitt who had greatly troubled her life, the home of her employer, Chief Inspector Coffin, who troubled her equally but differently. Could you feel anything significant for an older man? She thought she could, and that frightened her.

'And the Pitts?'

'Nice as well,' she responded cautiously.

He looked at her cup. 'Some more coffee?'

'I ought to get back to work.'

'Let's take a walk. And you can tell me about the Pitts.' He was going to write fiction, and to write fiction you had to gather facts about life: tales, emotions, relationships. And a triple death was something. He sensed she was in a position to tell him.

The Polytechnic enclosed a small square garden which the architect had seen as a kind of cloister for scholarly pacing. There wasn't much of that done in it, but a good deal of rendezvousing and sitting in the sun. The grass in the centre was consequently beaten down and dry.

She nodded nervously, not sure why.

'Like another roll to take out?' He was going to have one himself. He hoped she chose ham, they were the best.

She nodded again, feeling exactly like Weenie. 'Ham, please.'

As they passed under the arch into the cloister, he said: 'Did you like the Pitts? I think you must have done.' Not quite true, Sarah thought, although I could see their good points. 'Did most people like them?'

'I don't know. I don't think I ever talked about them to anyone.' Except to Peter, of course, who had talked about them constantly. But even then, she had listened rather than talked back. They were a nuisance in her life and that was the truth of it. 'Admired, I suppose. Yes, I did admire them.'

'And other people? The neighbours and people in the shops, did they admire them?'

'Well, they might have done. They had a beautiful car, always had lovely clothes, and looked so good. Got things right somehow.'

'Envious, was that it?'

'I wasn't envious.' Not true. She had been very envious of Nona, even of Irene.

'My dad thinks it's because they were what they were that they were killed.'

'But that's terrible.' She wasn't as shocked as she pretended to be, though; it was likely that was the way it had been.

'Didn't fit in. Successful, when they would have done better not to be so successful. Or not to show it. Too much money for round here. Wrong school for the children, wrong clothes, wrong car. Showing themselves different.' As well as politics and economics, he read sociology. 'They should have merged. But they stood out.'

'They couldn't help it.'

'Wouldn't have mattered in Chelsea or Hammersmith, but round here... wrong.'

Sarah finished her ham roll.

'So what do you want from me?'

'Any ideas who it could be?'

'No, of course not.' And I wouldn't tell you if I had. Entirely too high a price for a bit of ham and bread.

'My dad thinks it's what he calls a "neighbourhood" crime. Some person noticed them and hated them for what they were.'

'What you're saying is: they deserved to be killed.'

'I'm not saying that,' he said, as if he might not be, but someone else might.

'I don't think the police ought to talk like that.' John Coffin, she felt sure, would not; he might think the same things, but would not say them in that way.

She wiped her mouth clean of the little bit of fat from the ham. 'I must be off home. I have to see my brother.' The moment she thought of Peter, then Martin (no, she would not think of him in the ridiculous way with a small m) no longer looked so good, so handsome. Not a patch on Peter.

She rushed into the house, throwing her books on a chair. Peter was lying back on the sofa, doing nothing in particular.

'You're back early.'

'I've left you alone too much. I left you on your own all day yesterday.'

He averted his eyes. 'Yesterday I had Weenie,' he said with a hint of irony. 'She was sick because she ate too much. Today she's back at school. I dare say she will be sick again tomorrow. I expect she'll try to be.'

'You say horrible things.'

'I've got horrible lately.'

'And that's true.' But she excused him, as she always excused all of them, except herself. Only she herself knew the evil thoughts she had and how effortlessly they could be translated into action. 'I'll make a cup of tea.'

No, she would not tell Peter that the person he loved most in the world was dead. Someone he loved more than he loved her, which was a hard pill to swallow. Not that she was jealous, she just thought that Nona had too much of everything. In the scales of life Nona was right up, and the Flemings down, down, down. Now the girl was gone. And Sarah knew, while Peter didn't. It amazed her that she should find it difficult to tell him. If anyone had said to her yesterday that it would be almost beyond her powers to tell Peter of Nona's death, she would have laughed. As easy as eating pie, she would have said. She knew better now.

Then she saw that Peter had been crying and that he had taken the trouble to wear a clean, white shirt. White could be a colour of mourning, and cleanliness probably was too. So somehow or other, he knew.

She carried the tea back in, hot and sweet in big mugs. There was some gingerbread as well. 'Who told you?'

He did not attempt to deny it. 'Went for a walk. Saw a policeman outside No. 22. People standing staring. Something was wrong. I asked.' And then: 'How do you know?'

'Someone at the Poly.' You wouldn't think lightning could strike in the same place twice would you? But apparently with Nona it could. Death had really gone looking for her.

THERE WAS A CROWD now in Church Row. Mr Brocklebank, who had been sent by his wife to look at the house, reported back. He said what Sarah Fleming had been thinking.

'Poor unlucky kid. You wouldn't think it could happen twice.'

'It's the house,' said his wife sombrely.

'Now cut that out, old girl.'

She ran through the record. All the deaths in the past, some were history, those were painless, but not the new ones. The student, William Egan, all the Pitt family. No, it was no joke.

He did not dispute her catalogue. 'Never said it was a joke. Not one to laugh at, at least.' There were occasionally cosmic jokes, you all felt the force of those, they were masked by the words, war, earthquake, or air crash, and this might be one of them. He had a pious sense of his own importance and had always thought all these acts were directed at him, from which he had only escaped by good luck. 'You ought to tell the police. Nothing to do with what's happened now, of course, I'm not saying that, but you ought to tell them.' His voice was coaxing. 'Let me telephone that policeman you work for. Get him to come to you here. He's a decent sort, he'll do it and then you can talk to him.'

She thought it over. 'No. I ought to go down to the police station. It would be more suitable.'

'Are you up to it. Rhoda?'

But she thought she was. 'If you come with me.'

Ben Brocklebank was a tall, well-built man, but his wife was as tall and nearly as sturdy. Side by side, a matching pair, both in their best clothes, they set off for the police station on Royal Hill.

She took his arm. 'There was nothing really wrong in what I did, Ben.'

'Of course not, Rhoda.'

'Just taking a liberty. Nothing worse. I'm glad I told you all about it at the time. That sets me right with myself.'

Before she left she had gone into her kitchen, os-
tensibly to lock the back door, but in fact to look at
her new refrigerator, her automatic washing-machine
and her food-mixer. She had a new sink and new
bright yellow cabinets to go with them. She had given
the food-mixer a pat; it was the new object she loved
best. She had never used it.

Royal Hill police headquarters was housed in a new
building. Opened last year, it had been designed by an
architect who was a follower of the new brutalism in
architecture for which a police building gave full
scope. It was an uncompromising block which looked
as though it could withstand a siege. The set of rooms
assigned to the TAS unit was at the rear with its own
entrance and allocated car parking. Offered to allow
them a kind of autonomy, Coffin knew it had been
meant originally as a Traffic Inquiry Unit. It was furnished with a certain meanness of equipment that
made them feel like poor relations. Coffin was fighting hard for all he needed, but cuts and economies
were the rule of the day, and this was 1978 and no one
liked the police.

He was surprised to see Mrs Brocklebank and
slightly more surprised to see Ben Brocklebank whom
he had never absolutely believed in before, thinking
him more an excuse than a man, someone Mrs B.
sheltered behind when it suited her not to do something.

He listened to what she had to say. 'So you hid William Egan in No. 22? Exactly why did you do that?'
He was not disposed to be easy with her.

She muttered something about knowing him all her life, and he hadn't got any money. Come out of prison and look for a living in 1978? Well, you couldn't. He hadn't a penny to his name.

'So he came to you and said can you put me up and you did?' asked an unfeeling Coffin. 'Pretty generous-minded of you. With your employer's property.'

So now he knew where the mouse droppings had come from on Egan's clothes. From the basement of the Pitt house. And that was why he had dirty boots from the road works in Church Row. He had walked in the muck. Just as Coffin had himself, and others too for all he knew. (Sarah Fleming could have confirmed this from her observation of the boots of Weenie and Co.)

'I didn't know where else to put him.'

He had something on her, he thought. A weak woman who looked strong, he thought. Blackmail, that had the mark of William Egan. But he would not find out more while the husband was there. Was she the third person, whose presence he had always sensed?

She muttered something about him paying what he could.

'Oh, so he did pay something?'

'You didn't tell me that, Rhoda,' said Ben Brocklebank alertly.

'It wasn't much.'

'And what did you do with it?'

'Yes,' said Coffin. 'What did you?'

'I had a little debt.' She did not meet his eyes. 'I was clearing it off.'

A lie? Or part of the blackmail?

'And then I found out,' said Ben. 'Caught the old girl with a bottle of whisky in her bag. What's this? I said. Who's on the bottle?'

'So you went round and turned him out?'

'Well, no. By that time he'd upped and gone. Left a note saying the mice were getting him down. And that night he was killed.'

So he had probably left exactly when he meant to leave, intending to attack Terry Place but being killed himself.

'All that rigmarole about the house being a haunted house was just to keep people from inquiring if they saw any signs of William Egan's habitation?' Infestation, he nearly said.

'Perhaps I put it on a bit, but that's a bad house.' She spoke earnestly. 'And I mean it.'

'Now don't go back to that, old girl,' said Ben. 'Just forget talk like that. She's not herself,' he said, turning to Coffin. 'But no one could call it a lucky house, could they?'

'No.' Coffin turned to Mrs Brocklebank. 'You had a bad shock. How are you now?'

'I'm not thinking about it. Trying not to. I still keep seeing them, though. And it had a sort of smell, that room. I can still smell it... Do you know how they died yet, sir?'

'It was probably poison.' He could tell her that much, and he owed it to her to say something. She had cleared up a few worrying points about William Egan.

Then he had a thought. 'Did you know Terry Place too?'

She nodded.

'Well?'

She shook her head.

'Roxie's your friend, isn't she?' said Ben, who seemed determined to open up channels in Coffin's mind. 'Thick as thieves.'

'It must have been difficult for you, hiding Egan when Place was living with his sister.'

'I never said and she never said. We know when to keep quiet.'

So you do, thought Coffin, so you do. The interlinked circles of this part of London, declining and changing now as social patterns altered and moved people away, but still strong in those groups which had gone to school together, married within their peer group and worked side by side, struck him afresh.

But I'm one of them, he thought. Look at me now, back here, and with Rhoda Brocklebank working for me. It was really better to be like Paul Lane, about as rootless as you could be, moving easily around as served your ambition and owing no one anything.

Perhaps he and Laetitia should forget their search for their missing brother or sister, who, after all, might not want to be found, and let the past look after itself?

There was the younger generation, the Flemings, they were another case of it; they certainly had their roots here, but they were different again. Sarah Fleming would break away. Brains and education and character would do it for her. She was bent on it.

Perhaps a community like this resented outsiders and would always try to throw them out? Was this what had happened with the Pitts? But there was another factor in their case, as he was well aware.

He had had Bernard Jones on the telephone muttering about a 'neighbourhood' crime and he had found the idea disquieting. To accept it required a whole sociology of crime. But perhaps he preferred it to a haunted house, because, as he saw it, that would require metaphysics as well.

'You go on home,' he said to Rhoda Brocklebank. 'Don't bother to come in to work tomorrow.' It was one of her days for him.

'Oh, I'm going to.' She had given up calling him 'sir', he noticed. 'I'll come to you and glad to, but never to that other house. Never again.'

She saw a haunted house, a superstition she had perhaps used for her own account, and he saw something more human, a complex web of relationships, interlocking and interacting in a way he could not yet fathom, and in which people got caught up and destroyed. She was thinking about the Pitts, and he was thinking about his sister.

Paul Lane came into the room just as he had finished telephoning Laetitia. His third telephone call of the day to her, she needed his words.

'It was potassium cyanide. Powder form. In the soup. Curry soup would hide the taste until it was too late. How and when it got in there we don't know as yet. Could have been an accident.'

'Irene Pitt was planning to cook curry soup,' said Coffin. 'Told me so herself, I met her and she told me. She made the curry powder herself.'

'Then she may have taken the poison for one of the spices. Mistaken it somehow.'

'She was going to shop for spices in Greenwich Market. I told her it was a good place.'

'Well, we'll ask. It's a start.'

ROXIE FARMER and Shirley Place, unlikely sisters-in-law, were under one roof for the time being. They were sitting in the kitchen over a cup of tea. There was no pretence of grief on either side for the death of William Egan or the predicament of Terry Place. As far as the women were concerned, they had wiped each other out and that was that.

'While they needed us, we did what we could,' said Shirley. 'As far as we could.'

Their eyes met. Roxie assented: 'As far as we could.' They understood each other.

'You had your Terry here when he got out, and I'm grateful to you because if it hadn't been you, it would have had to be me, and with Dad the way he was, I was better out of the country. He'd have beat me up as well as Terry if he could. I'm sorry he had to go the way he did, but it was always going to happen, the sort of man he was. Dad, I used to say, you are your own worst enemy and someone'll kill you for it one day. Of course I didn't think it would be Terry when I married him. You don't think of things like that on your wedding day.'

'No,' Roxie nodded. She never talked as much as Shirley. 'Another cup?'

'If you like, dear.'

The kitchen was bright and newly furnished with the best of domestic equipment. Dishwasher, automatic washing-machine, a luxury freezer, even Rhoda Brocklebank hadn't got more.

'You've got this place lovely.' Shirley stirred her tea. A crocodile handbag lay on the table and she had just slipped off her new Italian shoes. 'You're the home-making type. I'm more of a party girl, myself.'

'Mmm.'

'But I don't think it matters what you are, as long as you've got the money to do it.'

From where she sat, Shirley could see the street. 'Oh look, visitors. Now that's a car full of cops, if ever I saw one.'

Roxie looked and saw Chief Inspector Coffin and Inspector Lane. 'I think they've come to see you.' She felt quite calm after her talk with Shirley, who was a good sort, if rough. 'After they've gone, shall we have our little bonfire?'

It was a routine call on the bereaved Mrs Place who had lost her father and who might soon be a widow, who had perhaps shed a few tears, but not very many.

Yet it was Shirley Place who kept the interview firmly null and void. No, she couldn't help them at all.

She had been away on a little holiday in Spain and knew nothing. A total shock. Yes, she was very shocked. Hardly knew how to conduct herself, but Roxie was being so kind.

Yes, it was terrible what her husband had done, and she couldn't explain it. He had been a violent man and her father had been a man even more violent, it was a pity they had ever met.

'They met in prison,' Coffin reminded her sharply, 'apart from anywhere else.'

A deep breath and a pat with her handkerchief at her eyes. Roxie looked more grieved than she did, much more. There was a heart in Roxie somewhere.

As they left, Coffin said to Paul Lane: 'I'd like to know what they were talking about when we got there. Something was going on.'

'Is there anything more to go on? Egan is dead, Place killed him. We'll probably get a confession if he ever comes round. End of case.'

'Oh, you're such a realist, Paul. You're sometimes so busy looking at the wood that you don't smell the trees are rotten.'

'I'm not sure I know what you mean.'

'I'm not sure I know myself.'

But there was that house in his mind, he was building it again, putting room after room. It was getting to be as big as a cathedral.

No, not a cathedral, nothing like a cathedral. A great chambered tomb.

SEVEN

'AND WHAT IS IT that's so rotten?' Paul Lane was showing a mild aggression. Sometimes he found his boss's utterances too cryptic. Coffin the seer. In one of his Delphic moods, he told himself, which was unfair, since the boss must sometimes puzzle himself as much as his underlings.

They were driving away from Roxie Farmer's house through Marlowe Street, one of the meaner streets of Greenwich. A high-rise block of flats had been clamped down on a street that did not think well of itself at the best of times. Paradise Street, next to Decimus Street and round the corner from the area known as the 'Dirty Wick', was a hard place to call home. The flats had been built ten years earlier and showed wear badly. The pale cement-coloured walls were streaked with dirt like snot running from a thousand noses. Here and there old cars littered the streets like debris from a civil war.

Coffin answered: 'Just what's rotten I don't know. But there is a little something I can detect in the atmosphere between those two that might or might not have something to do with the murder of Egan by Place.'

The streets seemed dirtier here than anywhere else, dirtier even than normal, with paper, empty beer cans and dog dirt distributed lavishly on the pavement and gutters. There was a street market here at weekends, and a few days ago there had been a fair to celebrate some local festival. Hygiene was never high on the priorities of Marlowe Street.

'But whatever it is, it can have nothing to do with the death of the Pitts.' Paul Lane was driving, and far too fast as was his wont.

'It has something to do with all these lives. It's part of the background.'

Now that was not the way for a modern police officer to speak, Lane felt.

The car swung round a corner into the dusty main road. A large new foodmarket was being built on the opposite corner, with the land around it open for parking. The line of small shops across the way already looked depressed by the opposition. One or two were empty. A bakery had become a betting shop and a draper's had turned into the offices of a building society.

'So you do believe in a "community crime"?' Lane preferred this way of putting it. Neutral, euphemistic, alliterative, you distanced yourself from the idea of neighbours killing each other. Anyway, it didn't happen like that, and Coffin knew it. That sort of killing was done by lighted petrol thrown through a window, or a kicking to death in a dark street.

'No. It's not the business of the TAS squad to prove a community crime.'

'So what is?'

'Oh, I don't know.' Coffin made an irritable response. Usually calm and reflective, he was showing tension. Laetitia came into it, he found himself thinking about her. 'To show that crimes happen to people for a valid motive and a valid despair, not just prejudice. Not the colour, race, religion or class of the victim as the triggering factor.' Did he believe it? 'Watch that bus,' he said sharply, as Lane shot forward.

The neighbourhood changed about here as a stream of heavy traffic turned towards the old Woolwich Arsenal, depression on one side and the beginning of suburban prosperity on the other. A wine bar and a smart hairdresser marked the divide. Lane did not take offence at his boss's comment, nor did he slow down. The bus swung away, unscathed.

'Well, I hope you are right. Has it struck you that you could be wrong?'

'Yes.' A bleak admission. 'All the time.'

EIGHT

IT WAS THE SORT of night on which questions would not go away. Something of the atmosphere in Roxie Farmer's house seemed to go home with Coffin and give him a restless night. He had his own worries: there was going to be an official inquiry into the shooting on the arrest of Terry Place. But Terry was now conscious and might possibly admit that he had fired first.

He went into his kitchen to make a pot of tea. The kitchen was tiny, but newly furnished and painted. As he stood waiting for the kettle to boil, he reflected that he had nothing so good and lavish as he had observed through the open door of Mrs Farmer's kitchen. Good stuff there. The same with Mrs Place's clothes. Interesting that both women seemed to have had access to more money than you would expect. A problem with Mrs Brocklebank and money too. Now he considered, it was the signs of money spent, taken together with some looks exchanged between Roxie and her sister-in-law, that had worried him.

Those three women knew each other and knew two victims of violence and one of them, his own Mrs Brocklebank, knew all five. She even had thoughts about a sixth person who had died. Malcolm Kincaid. What about asking some questions?

He poured the tea, strong and thick, the way he liked it. Automatically, his hand went out for a chocolate biscuit.

Then he started to think about the other case, the poisoning of a whole family group at No. 22, Church Row. Questions, questions again. The whole of his work depended on asking the right questions. How much was he getting wrong?

If it was not a community crime, if the Pitts had not been slaughtered because they stood out from their fellows in a way the neighbourhood resented, then why had they died?

And who was the killer?

Coffin listed the possible people.

The husband.

The lover.

The wife.

Or some other person, unknown.

That made it a crime within the family. Murder and then suicide. There was also the daughter, but he exempted her. He could not see Nona Pitt as the poisoner of her parents. Interesting that the boy had been spared. Was that significant? But then, of course, he had not been at home. So chance played a part in the mass murder, did it? Those who happened to eat that meal died.

Was the killer an outsider, then? A person whose identity was not yet known to him and whose very existence remained to be proved.

With what motive? Or was it going to prove one of those motiveless crimes that strangely surfaced every now and then? He thought of the seventeenth-century poisoner, Madame de Brinvilliers, who had run round the hospitals of Paris poisoning people for 'practice'. Practice was a motive of a kind. Was it one here?

But this was all speculation. Let the evidence lead the way. He considered the evidence. The forensics, for much of which he was still waiting, and might go on waiting unless he pressed, the photographs and diagrams contained in the Scene of Crime report, and the testimony of Mrs Brocklebank. Not much.

He knew the man in charge of the case and had asked (as head of the TAS) to be kept in touch with developments. He didn't think he would be.

But that worked both ways. He might not do much talking back himself.

He might urge Lane to pick up what he could, Lane was a great scrounger of information.

The telephone rang.

Christopher Court, MP, had no difficulty in getting straight through on the telephone to Chief Superintendent Coffin once he had decided it was to him he wished to speak. Being an MP still carried some weight; he was PPS to a powerful minister at Defence, and the threat of the General Election had rolled away for the time being: he was someone to heed.

'Hello? Chris Court here.' He was always polite and easy on the telephone. It was a learned skill. 'Chief Inspector? We met briefly at the Pitts' party. That last party.'

'I remember.' John Coffin was in his office crouched in the imitation Bauhaus chair which did not really accommodate his bulk and certainly did not offer the comfort it promised. He was doing three tasks at once: checking the statements of witnesses in a report being prepared for the Public Prosecutor and at the same time turning over the photographs and diagrams of the house in Church Row which the SOCO had put together. He was staring at a photograph of the whole dead group. In colour. Those were two jobs. The third was to talk to the man who had been in love with Irene Pitt.

'I know your sister. We met in New York.'

'Laetitia? Half-sister.' Why did he say that? He didn't have to explain Letty. He might have had to explain his mother's activities, but she was dead. In a brief space of time, she had scattered offspring around the country and omitted to let any of them know each other. A real wanderer, and he looked for a sign of her inheritance in himself. Couldn't find any, unless bad luck with love and marriage was one. Come to think of it, it probably was.

'I'd like to talk to you.'

'Yes, certainly, Mr Court. Would you like to drop in? Name your time.'

'Oh, Christopher, please. Could you come here? Whitehall Court?'

'Right.' See a man in his own background, you learn something about him.

'Only thing is: I share this flat with another MP.' He sounded nervous. 'Still, he's not here at the moment.'

'It'd have to be this evening. I'm afraid. Can't get away before.'

Coffin had a desk full of work. But he could not take his eyes off the photograph in front of him. There was something about it that tugged for attention.

'Could it be . . . not exactly unofficial, but will you have to bring another officer with you?'

'I can come on my own.' Coffin kept his voice non-committal. 'I couldn't pass over anything you told me, though.'

'Of course not. Wouldn't want it. Come and have a bite with me. I'm not bad on grilling a steak.' Chris Court's voice was lighter, as if now he had got the conversation under way, he felt better. Coffin wondered what he had to say. As far as he knew, the MP had not been interviewed about the case. Not that his name had been kept out exactly. At least once a gossip columnist had run a story about 'the lonely and about to be divorced MP for Roundhead East' in a column next to the story about Irene Pitt and her husband. You could read between the lines and many would. He flipped over the pages of the report he was reading. No, the MP had not been visited, but his name was mentioned. He went back to the photograph.

'I'll do that.' They fixed a time. Not too late, Chris Court said, as he would have to listen for the Division bell and might have to run for it.

Coffin's eye rested on a detail in the photograph. He forgot, momentarily, about the MP and what he might have to say. Now he knew what he found interesting in it.

The soup tureen was in front of Edward Pitt, the curving silver ladle on the table by his plate. He had served the soup himself. He must have been the last to drink it. He might even have been standing up as he tasted the first mouthful. First mouthful, last mouthful.

Had he been watching the others, before he took his own spoonful?

Coffin thought he would be glad to have the full post-mortem results on each body to know exactly how much poison was inside each stomach. They had all taken enough to kill, that was sure.

Strange way to commit murder and then suicide, he reflected, putting potassium cyanide in the curry soup. Mask the flavour, of course.

Which did seem to point to someone who knew about the curry soup being prepared for supper. Someone who could get at the soup, too.

IT WAS a smoky hot evening when the two men met, but the flat where the MP lived was cool and dark. If he shared it with someone there was no sign of the other man; but perhaps the whole place was rented furnished and what Coffin could see, heavy leather sofas and hunting prints, was some third party's scheme of decoration. Court destroyed this idea as he poured out drinks.

'My wife did the flat. She's an interior decorator. I think she was having a joke at my expense when she did it.' He sounded weary. 'She knows I'm allergic to horses and can't fire a gun.'

Coffin took his drink, which was comfortably cool in the glass. 'Has it been done long?' The furnishings did not look new, but elegantly worn and homely. But perhaps that was the effect aimed at.

'About five years.' Court took up his own drink. The marriage must have been in trouble even then, he thought, and he hadn't known. You never read the signals right. But in the final analysis it had been he who wanted out.

To John Coffin's eye the other man still seemed nervous. This was interesting since he was on Coffin's list of suspects.

He waited. Court plunged straight in, with the air of someone getting something disagreeable over. 'I was going to marry Irene. I suppose you knew that?'

'I did.' Laetitia had told him, apart from the general gossip on the subject.

'We had agreed to wait until they all came back from the States.' He was still speaking jerkily. 'I didn't want that. Naturally. But it was the way it was.'

'You're still married?'

'Yes. As you obviously already know.' Coffin nodded, without speaking. 'The arrangement suited my wife. She's going to remarry too. It was all quite friendly. Or I thought it was. I thought it was what Edward Pitt wanted.' He got up and started to walk around the room. Obviously he had come to the heart of what he wanted to say. 'But when they came back from New York, Edward was quite different. Hostile.

Angry.' He took some of his drink as if it was bitter in his mouth. 'Of course, you can never tell with people like that.'

Coffin said nothing. Can't you indeed, he thought. If Edward Pitt picked up that in you, no wonder he was angry.

'He wasn't going to let go easily. I don't think he was going to let Irene come to me.'

'Was anything said?'

'No, Irene said I was imagining things. I don't think so. I didn't like his mood. I told her so, but she just laughed. Said she could handle him.'

'Is that all?'

'She admitted he was quarrelling with her. Nastily, she said, and he had never been that before. And then of course all this business with the girl complicated things.'

'Are you telling me that you think Edward Pitt killed his family?'

'I'm saying that I think he could have done.'

Coffin considered. After all, Edward Pitt's name was on his own private list of suspects. But so too was that of Court himself. 'Got anything more definite than mere feeling?'

Through the open window floated the sound of traffic, and then above this the boom of Big Ben sounding the hour.

'I'll just get us something to eat. Are you hungry? I am.'

In a housewifely kind of way, Court went out to the kitchen, returning with a plate of sandwiches. 'Brown bread with smoked salmon, white bread with turkey. Sorry not to produce steak, but I didn't have time.'

He grinned, suddenly looking younger. 'We owe these to Bob Mackintosh who shares this flat with me. His girlfriend runs a catering business.'

Coffin took a sandwich and waited. He was getting to know the way this man worked. In a second or two he would come out with something. Might be good material, might not. He took a bite: the turkey was smoked also.

'Yes, there was something.' Court also took a sandwich, he held it in his hand. 'Funny, isn't it? Smoking cigarettes is bad for you, but anything smoked to eat is fine. All right. He was interested in poisons. I saw a book on poisons on his library table the day of that party where we met. You were there with your sister.'

'Letty and I met there. Surprise to me.' He got out a notebook. 'Tell me the name of this book.'

'*The Book of Poisons* by Gustave Schenk.' It wasn't much, but it was something. 'I'll check to see if it's still there.'

'He'd been reading it. Well, someone had.'

'To wipe out almost your whole family suggests someone in an abnormal state of mind.'

'He wasn't normal, no.'

Coffin wished he had observed Edward Pitt more closely on that evening, but he had been so taken up with Letty.

'I am sure Irene was coming round to knowing that. She was more and more worried. And then she had the worry about Nona.'

'Yes, that was a bad business. You think it contributed to Edward Pitt's state of mind?'

'Irene was worried about the girl before that happened. It was part of it. The reason they decided to send the girl away, but Irene had something else on her mind.'

'Did she tell you what?'

'She told me something. It was something connected with three students who rented their house some years ago.'

Coffin raised his head alertly.

'She asked me to inquire about the case. She thought I might know the right channels.'

'She could have asked me.'

Court shrugged. 'She wanted to know more about the student who killed himself.'

'Malcolm Kincaid?'

'That was the name. He poisoned himself.'

The words dropped into the room, like hard pebbles.

'So he did,' said Coffin.

'Irene had an idea, I don't know where she got it from, that a child, or a young person, came into the case somehow. She asked me to find out. I did. One of my research assistants did some investigation. And yes, the police did think that a young person, sex unknown, had been on the scene of the suicide. Fiona, that's my assistant, was not told any more. I passed it on to Irene.'

'Where did Mrs Pitt get this idea about the child?'

Court shrugged.

'And what did she say when you told her what your assistant had found out?'

'Not much. I suppose she meant Nona. But she did not actually admit it. Could have been the boy. All Irene said to me was that what worried her was that "she had said nothing to her". It must have been Nona.'

The figure of the dead girl seemed to move before them.

'She was a beautiful girl,' said Coffin. 'What was she like?'

'I hardly got to know her,' he said quickly, looking away. 'She was a child when they went off, and then grew up quickly in New York. Or that was the way it seemed. But she had character, and if she had a secret, I would say she could keep it.'

They finished their drinks and almost silently ate their way through the plate of sandwiches.

'I'll find out what the local police know,' said Coffin as he left.

'I expect they know more than they told Fiona.'

'Probably. But thanks for telling me all this.'

'It may mean nothing. But I wanted you to know.'

For the first time, Coffin saw the signs of grief on Christopher Court's face.

So COFFIN WENT back and early next day started his own questions. He went straight to Bernard Jones. He had something to discuss with Paul Lane, but Jones first about the Kincaid death.

He got Jones on the telephone and at home. A young voice answered the telephone, a lad, but willingly went away to get his father. Bernard had had his breakfast but had not yet turned his mind to the day. A process which went slowly these days. By the sound of it, he was in the middle of shaving. So Coffin had to work on him a bit first to get him to think laterally. Or to think at all.

'Oh, you're on about that again? Don't know why it interests you so much.'

Coffin was silent. Why he was interested was his own affair at the moment. If Bernard came across with anything good, then he would go to the archives and read the files himself.

'Yes,' said Bernard, dragging in the recesses of a memory which, like his stomach, was capacious but had to be treated carefully. 'Yes, I remember now. There was some talk of a kid having disturbed the body. Nothing to do with the suicide, of course, just having been there. Probably the first person to discover the body.'

'What was the evidence?' It might not be important to him, but he wanted to know.

'Think it was sweetpapers and a comic dropped at the scene. We thought it indicated a youngster.'

'Yes,' said Coffin thoughtfully. He would consult the archives himself, thinking over what Bernard had recalled.

Which was almost accurate, and almost enough. But when Coffin checked in the records, intact but dusty, he found that the comic was not a comic but a girls' magazine. One aimed at the teenage market. And the sweetpapers were not sweetpapers but the cover from an expensive brand of chocolate. Someone had not been very intelligent, he thought.

It could have been the Pitt girl.

Malcolm Kincaid had died from potassium cyanide. And so had the Pitts.

Had the girl found the poison, kept it, and then used it? Or, if she had kept it, had someone else in that family, possibly the father, come by it and used it? Which of them had been reading *The Book of Poisons?*

It was a question to ask, and no doubt this time, one which should be asked. Answering would be something else again.

Meanwhile, he had other questions on that strangely linked case of the murder of William Egan by his son-in-law, Terry Place.

Nothing was certain. They might yet discover that someone else was guilty, but he did not think so. Terry it was, but he wished the man would come round and answer questions. One of them, anyway, he could put to Lane.

This, with other and routine business, took him half a morning, during which Inspector Lane was out of the office on other business and the two young sergeants were in and out all the time; they seemed to work as a unit. Lane had his own small office but was rarely to be found in it.

Early in the afternoon he heard his voice and went in to put his question. 'Oh yes, money,' said the Inspector briskly. 'I'm glad you're asking. I've been wondering about that myself. Yes, both Place and Egan had considerable sums stowed away from various jobs. Or they should have had, because we never laid our hands on it. Even allowing for what they would have lost on laundering the proceeds, there should have been a tidy sum. I've been wondering where it was now.' Which meant that he had been giving it considerable quiet thought. 'There weren't many people that pair trusted.'

'I thought my memory hadn't played me wrong.' He clearly remembered noting the size of Egan's haul. 'Especially about Bill Egan.'

'Oh yes. That was why he had it in for you for putting him away. He got a long sentence. All that lovely money and he couldn't touch it. But, as it happened, he got out a bit sooner than expected. Quite a bit sooner. That must have been a shock to Place.'

'Yes, he saved that warder.'

'That's right, and got his sentence reduced for doing it. Although I did hear that accident wasn't entirely kosher.'

'The warder bought a new house, has he?'

'He may have been hoping to. No luck there now with Egan gone.'

'He might try Mrs Egan.'

Lane just laughed.

'Whom did those two men trust? Would Egan have left it with his daughter?'

'Doubt it. Not much love lost there.'

'What about Terry Place, would he trust his wife?'

'No, but he'd trusted his sister.'

'And Egan seems to have trusted Rhoda Brockle-bank.'

'So he did.'

'And Rhoda Brocklebank and Roxie Farmer and Shirley Place have all been spending money,' said Coffin. 'With a free hand.'

The two men stared at each other.

'I suggest we talk with all these three women. I'll take Rhoda Brocklebank,' said Coffin. 'And you can have the other two.'

So that could be one little mystery rolled up.

If he got the answers he expected, that Rhoda had kept William Egan's money in some hiding place and that Roxie had been looking after her brother's moneybags, and that all three women had been spending what they were supposed to be hoarding, then he knew what was causing the atmosphere he had picked up at Roxie's house.

It was hard guilt.

AT THIS POINT the young sergeant, David Evans, strolled into the room. He had been keeping a watch on Terry Place at the hospital. There was a uniformed constable by the bed all the time, but David Evans was hanging about as an unofficial extra. He was not exactly made welcome, but it was recognized that the TAS outfit had an interest.

'He's come round,' he announced. He was excited, but not wishing to show it.

'And?'

'He more or less admits that he fired first.'

'What does that mean?' demanded Coffin.

'He says he'd won the right to kill.' The sergeant added: 'He thinks he'd dying. I think it puts you in the clear. He's admitting it was his fault.'

'Good,' said Paul Lane.

'You can't win the right to kill,' said Coffin. 'In what kind of a game do you win a death as a prize? What does he mean?'

Sergeant David Evans shrugged. 'Kind of Russian roulette, maybe. Doesn't have to be a real game. Mind's gone a bit, I suppose. Still, he said it.'

'You'd better get back and go on listening.'

'Topper's there, sir.' Geoffrey Topper was the other young sergeant.

'Well, we'll have to hope Place says something else.' But Coffin was pleased. He was off the hook. One other problem had rolled away.

But Evans had something more to say.

'Place came out with something funny, sir. I didn't know if I was hearing right. He said that there was a curse on the Pitts.'

'But he was unconscious by the time the Pitts died. How did he know anything about them?' Or what did he know?

The sergeant shrugged. 'Search me.'

'Don't say he killed them too.'

'He may just have meant the girl,' pointed out Lane.

'Sounded more general than that,' said Evans, who was enjoying his moment. 'As if he meant the whole lot of them.'

'Did he know them?' queried Coffin sharply. 'Had he even met them?'

'No evidence that he had at all. Not that we can find, and he isn't saying. Except the girl, that day in the tunnel.'

'If he killed them, then how did he do it?' said Lane.

'By remote control?' The sergeant was a keen science fiction man and always ready to be open-minded.

'I wouldn't call Terry Place one of the great criminal minds of our century,' said Inspector Lane.

'I think you are both forgetting that the Pitts died by poison,' said Coffin.

You did not have to be there in person in order to kill by poison; in fact, you probably tried not to be. That was what a poisoning was: death by remote control.

Where did Terry Place come in, to play his part in that triple killing? What was this right to kill?

It was still infinitely more likely, to his mind, that the poisoner was one of the Pitt family. Possibly the girl, more likely the father.

So why did Terry Place start talking about them?

As soon as one set of questions were on the way to being answered, others seemed to take their place.

ALTHOUGH HE DID not know it, Roxie Farmer and her sister-in-law were having the bonfire they had promised themselves. It was a fine evening and all the gardens around them were deserted by their usual gardeners because of an important football match being shown on television.

'We'll do it now,' Roxie said. 'Get it over.'

'I'll be happy.' Mrs Terry Place was not a girl to show false sentiment, and she was not going to show it now. Roxie could do that if she so wished. 'Give me the match.'

It was quite a small affair, but they took advantage of the occasion to burn some of their old clothes, throwing them on the fire with gleeful cries of 'Rubbish'. They added Terry Place's clothes as well, Roxie shedding an obligatory tear as she did so, while her sister-in-law remained dry-eyed. It was her only concession to family feeling, which had been severely strained during Terry's stay with her after he came out of prison. They were counting on him not coming out of hospital. Ever.

On the fire, when the heart of it was red, went a square, brightly coloured cardboard box covered with black and crimson dragons, and strange symbols.

It writhed and curled in the fire as if it was alive.

They were glad to see it go. It was only an empty box.

No one told Coffin about the bonfire. Nor did any intuition, any extra sense, alert him to the fact that part of the case he was quietly and imperceptibly building up inside him was going up in smoke.

NINE

WHILE THE LADIES were fuelling their fire, in more
ways than one, John Coffin was taking a walk. It was
the end of his working day, and although not exactly
free of preoccupation (he would be telephoning Paul
Lane the moment he got in), he wanted some time to
himself. He was wearing the unobtrusive shabby
clothes with soft shoes that would allow him to plod
round the streets without being noticed. He liked to do
this occasionally, acting as an anonymous, unob-
served pair of eyes and ears.

He was saving Mrs Brocklebank for tomorrow. As
she advanced with the vacuum cleaner she had forced
him to buy, with her duster over her arm, and her
customary air of efficiency, he would say: 'Wait a
minute, Rhoda.'

Now he knew she was called Rhoda, he could make
a brave start. Before, she had slightly intimidated him.
Men have always been respectful of Hestia, the god-
dess of the hearth, easily intimidated by the mysteries
she manipulates so easily. John Coffin was no exception; a clever and practical man, he was unable to
manage his own electric oven. It was new and the
knobs were different, the old one he had known his
way about. The refrigerator was easy, you just opened
the door and put food in it until it looked like an ig-

loo inside, and then a pair of hands which might or might not be your own came along and cleared out the ice so that you could use it again. On such simple lines he conducted his life. It was one of the ways he showed his generation. All the young ones like Topper and Evans learned to cook at their mother's knee. Or their first live-in girlfriend taught them quickly.

Now the capable Mrs Brocklebank had become someone who had a conscience and a guilty secret. She had told him half of her worry, but the other half she had kept to herself. She was just a subject to be questioned.

Today his walk did not hold his attention as it usually did. The streets were hot, the pavements sticky. No one was about except a black and white cat asleep in the sun. In the distance, through an open window, he could hear pop music pounding away, not the tune, if there was one, just the beat.

He turned into the main road that ran parallel with the unseen river. The district had changed since he last lived here, but he was not so old that he resented it. Change had to come, or we should all still be living in caves. Besides, in some ways the change was for the better.

In particular, Greenwich Wick was becoming a new world. Lurching into it, with one part lumbered with unlovely council tower blocks up the hill, while nearer the river the developers had arrived, and where once had been a network of tiny streets harbouring some of the most professional criminal families in South London, there were now several expensive blocks of flats:

expensive because they faced the river and looked sideways to the old Royal Palace of Greenwich with the trees and slopes of the park behind. Coffin wondered if the inhabitants of Drake Towers, with their BMWs and Porsches, knew that the old Francis Drake Street had been a regular thieves' kitchen. Policemen had walked in pairs there in the old days.

The joke was, as he knew from the records, that one or two of the most successful criminal families had moved from council flats into the new apartments on the proceeds of a life of profitable wrongdoing. Billy Egan and Terry Place had not quite risen to their ranks, although Egan at least had aspired to.

For a moment he found himself thinking of Letty. He had tried to telephone her twice and got no reply, not even an answering machine delivering a placatory little message. He began to suspect that she had gone to Glasgow. In which case he might even now have a new brother or sister. He wasn't sure he really wanted this, which was perhaps why he had not done much about it himself. He had Letty and now found himself dreading a new face to love.

He swung round and began to walk back to Church Row. He was not reading the district well this evening, he might as well give up and go home. He felt alien, not necessarily a bad thing in itself for an observer. A sense of detachment might produce a sharper view, but he felt unreal, as if the scene he was viewing was nothing more than a backdrop at a theatre which might roll itself up and disappear when the present act was over. It was fatigue, of course; that special feeling of unreality was nearly always due to weariness.

From out of the past came a memory of a quick cut home, down past the side of Deller's and then out into Queen Charlotte's Alley. Not a recognized route, it had been a track much used and he was willing to bet it was still there. An air of antiquity hung over that pathway, which, followed to its logical end, ran down to the river, as if the ancient Britons had used it first and it would go on being used even after the Bomb fell.

He found the path easily, broken at one or two points by the new arrangements at Deller's, a shed here, a car parked there, but both easily circumvented.

He was walking into Queen Charlotte's Alley before he recognized where he was. Coming at it, at this angle on this hot evening, he saw the change vividly. Now it was smart. In the old days, it had been just poor.

After all, he had not come here by accident. Give his unconscious mind a chance and it usually showed his feet which way to go.

He wanted to see Sarah Fleming. He wanted to see both the Flemings. They were the bridge between the two crimes.

Not Terry Place, who, as far as could be judged, had never met any of the Pitts except the girl, and that on a day that nearly killed him.

Not Rhoda Brocklebank, even though she knew everybody, and was certainly more deeply linked with

William Egan than she had admitted; not her because
she was not emotionally involved with the Pitts. They
were her employers, that was all. She had no insight to
offer him.

But the Flemings, yes, because Peter had certainly
loved Nona.

He knew Sarah was at home, since he could see her
watering the plants in her small garden. She was doing it with her usual spare, economical elegance, but
also with the air of one who would rather be doing
something else.

'You're not enjoying this,' he said, taking the heavy
can off her, and starting the watering himself.

'They are Weenie's plants, she put them in, the social worker said it would be good for her to have
something to look after, give her a sense of responsibility, but she doesn't do it.'

'Perhaps she'd do better with a cat or a dog.'

'One couldn't trust an animal to Weenie.'

'She'll grow up one day.'

'Oh yes, I expect she will, there's quite a lot of
growing inside Weenie. I don't know about the boys,
though.'

For a long time he had wondered about the history
of this little family, now it looked as though he was
going to find out.

'Weenie was with my mother and father when they
were killed, the boys weren't. Weenie would be normal enough, I think, if it weren't for that. She was all
right before. What happened then seemed to . . . stunt
her. Every way, physically and mentally. I don't think

the boys ever did have far to go, but Weenie did have.'
Her tone was sad.

'What happened?' He had heard some talk about
an accident. People didn't seem to care to talk about
it much.

'You don't know? Most people round here know.
It's a kind of fable. Or a joke. Only they don't joke
much about death. And they're sorry for us. They are
kind round here, never think they are not.'

Coffin nodded, telling himself he might remember
this fact when people talked to him about 'neighbourhood' crimes. Only perhaps your face had to fit
to get the kindness, you had to belong. The Flemings
undoubtedly belonged.

'Dad was driving the van. He hired it out. That was
how he made a living after he lost his job on the rail-
way, through drink and petty pilfering. I don't usually tell people that, although I expect you know
already. He was quite clever, Dad, in his way, but he
had never had an education. I don't think he wanted
it, he liked the way he was. Mum married beneath her,
as they say, she had an education, only it never took,
she wasn't bright. I used to wonder why she married
Dad, but I know really. It's easy. What they had in
common was what a lot of people have.'

She stopped, and then went on: 'Anyway, he had
Mum in the van with him and Weenie, but the rest of
us were at home. I was at school. He had a vanload of
manure. And he hit a lorry full of pigs going to the
abattoir at Woolwich.'

'Don't go on if you don't want to,' said Coffin.

'Dad hit the lorry, smashed right into it. And all the pigs came tumbling out. They found Dad in the middle of the road with a pig straddling him and manure all over his face. He was dead. So was the pig, for that matter. The rest of them were running round squealing. Weenie was all right, but Mum had a ruptured spleen and died before they could get her to hospital.'

'How long ago was this?'

'Nearly three years. I took over the family. Now you know why we are the way we are. You must have been wondering.'

Coffin thought she was gallant and brave and loving, when caring for Weenie and her brothers could not have come easily.

Sarah put the trowel she had been using carefully into her garden basket and removed her garden gloves. 'Why did you come tonight? Is it about your laundry? I know I've been slow lately. But there have been reasons.'

'I understand that, Sarah,' he said gently. 'And no, it's not about my laundry.' He picked up her basket. 'Shall we go into the house?'

She stood still. 'I know we must look a kind of circus.'

'Now, now.'

She allowed herself a small smile. 'Come on in, then, I'm going to make some coffee. Have a cup with me.'

The coffee proved to be filtered and freshly ground, something he had not expected.

She saw his expression and read it accurately. 'You expected coffee powder and boiling water, didn't you? Well, so it is most of the time. But this is my little luxury that I have when I can. When it seems the right time.'

He was pleased that this was the right time. He felt a warm liking for the pretty, brave girl. It might be a dangerous feeling, but he would see it was dangerous only to him and not to the girl.

They drank the coffee in the kitchen. No small talk, but a friendly silence.

'So why did you come?' Sarah put down her cup.

'Where is your brother?'

'Out walking. He mostly is, these days.' There was sympathy and toleration in her voice.

'He loved Nona?'

She nodded.

'What sort of a girl was she? How did you feel about her?'

'You mean, was she the sort of girl that other girls could be friends with? Yes, she was. Even a girl like me that would have liked some of the things she had. She was effortless, was Nona. Grown-up for her age, a bit wild. I envied her.'

'You don't need to.'

'I've always had to fight. I don't mind the fight. In a way I enjoy it. But just sometimes…' She shrugged. 'Well, poor kid, she's gone and I'm sorry. She didn't deserve that, none of them did.'

'Can you think of any reason why she should have been killed? Anyone who disliked her?'

Sarah shook her head silently. In a way, she had come close to hating Nona at times, although she was not going to admit it. But not to kill. Not like that.

'What about the rest of the family?'

She looked surprised. 'They were nice. Charming. I admired Irene. Didn't know Mr Pitt, but he was always polite.'

'Did everyone like them?'

She was silent again.

'Let me put that another way. Were they disliked as a family?'

She shook her head. 'No. They were nice people.'

Not exactly what I heard, thought Coffin.

'You never saw any signs of jealousy or resentment of them?'

Sarah occupied herself taking the coffee cups over to the sink. 'I know what you mean,' she said. 'But no, I never saw anything like that.'

'They were a lot richer than most people round here and had more status. Isn't that true?'

'Yes, yes and yes,' said Sarah, 'but I never saw any signs of hatred. There, have I answered you?'

'Yes. I think you have.' Coffin got up and stood looking out of the window. He could see a tiny backyard with a scrap of lawn and a few flowers. Clothes were pegged out on a line, nothing of his own. 'I would like to see your brother.'

'He'll be in. Or he won't be.' Another shrug.

'He recovered after that business down by the river? It was hard on him and the girl.'

'It was rotten for them. He was so brave and good then. He saved Nona's life.' Her voice was defiant.

Coffin said in a careful voice: 'Yes, but I find that the whole episode is puzzling. He knew Terry Place, didn't he?'

Sarah nodded, reluctantly, he felt, as if she would have denied it if she could. 'They both loved the *Cutty Sark,* and the river. I don't think Place can have been all bad, even if he did kill someone.'

'Friends, would you call them?' He was probing her. She knew something.

'Friends? That's a hard word. Only in a kind of way. They were people who had things in common.' She was phrasing it carefully, as if she was writing an essay. It alerted Coffin.

'Did he go there that day to meet Place? I have wondered. Coincidence worries me.'

'You'd have to ask him yourself.'

'And what do you think?'

Sarah hesitated. Then she took a deep breath. In the end you had to trust someone and she trusted this man. 'I'm not saying he knew Place would be there, but I guess he thought he would be.'

'Ah.' Coffin considered. 'Then why did he take the girl there?'

'He hasn't told me,' said Sarah carefully.

Coffin sat down again on one of the hard kitchen chairs. He would have to speak to the boy again. Get more out of him.

'He may have wanted to impress her,' said Sarah. 'Do something brave. And he did, of course. Or she

may have asked to go.' She dropped this into the conversation as an afterthought, but it interested Coffin.
Nona as an active participant in their arrival at the
tunnel party was a new idea.

'I'll have to speak to him myself.'

'I don't think anyone can talk to him at the moment. I know I can't. He doesn't seem to hear. The
doctor says it's shock. Because of Nona's death on top
of the other thing.'

'Is there anything else to tell me about Terry Place
and your brother?' He had the feeling there was
something more. It was in her eyes and the fidgety
movement of the hands.

After a moment of silence in which she studied his
face, she said: 'I don't know if it's of any importance,
but they played a game.'

'A game?' A fantastic picture of Terry Place with a
tennis racket came to him.

No, that was wrong. 'Bingo?'

'Not likely.' Sarah gave a small smile. 'A mind
game.'

'Like chess?' Even in fantasy he could not see Terry
Place settling down to a game of chess. Although he
could have learnt in prison.

'More like Snakes and Ladders.'

'Where did they play? Did they meet here?'

'I don't think they did meet. Or not much. Anyway, not here.' She was beginning to look harassed.
Leave the game, he told himself. Come back to it later.
For the moment he left the subject there, and went
back to another line of questioning.

'You say you did not know Nona Pitt well. I accept that. But you were the same age, you might have known or heard things about her that adults would not know.'

Sarah returned his gaze without much expression. He was coming to realize that she could hold her own under fire. Slowly she shook her head. 'Can't think of anything. We weren't at school together or anything like that.'

'But she was friendly with your brother even then.'

'Oh yes. Sure.' The ready, noncommittal agreement of her generation.

'Close? They were close?'

'Yes.' Now she smiled. 'Pete really did go for her then. That's when it began. For him anyway. Of course, she was only a kid. It couldn't be so important for her. She had a lot of growing to do.'

'It has been suggested to me that there was some episode in Nona's life that disturbed her, greatly disturbed her. And that it might have some bearing on what has happened now. I don't know what that episode was. Do you?'

'No.' She was telling the truth, he could tell.

'The name Kincaid mean anything to you? Malcolm Kincaid.'

She shook her head. 'No, not a thing. Never heard it.'

'He was one of the students who rented the Pitt house in Church Street, they were missing for a while. You never heard that story?'

'I seem to remember hearing something,' she said vaguely. 'But it didn't register.'

'Malcolm Kincaid was later found dead.'

'Oh.' The monosyllable reflected disinterested pity, no more. She might have said as much if a cat had died.

'What about your brother, would he know anything?'

'Is this in connection with Nona?'

'Yes, it is.'

'Then he might.' She corrected herself. 'Well, they were close.' She gave a little shake of her head. 'But if there was anything, then he never told me.'

'Might he have been involved? In whatever there was?'

Now she was wary. 'Peter never did anything wrong,' she said swiftly.

'I never said so.'

'Right.' She subsided.

'So you can't help me?'

'No. I never heard of anything. Nona always looked all right to me.'

She did not like the subject, he could see that. All the more reason to talk to Peter Fleming when he could.

He recognized a time to change tack. 'Any more coffee in the pot?'

Sarah shook it. 'A cup each.'

She had to put water in it to stretch it, but it was still a decent cup of coffee by his standards. Not by hers, though, he thought, watching her face as she drank.

A sudden wave of feeling for the clever, perfectionist girl washed over him.

'Your family are lucky to have you,' he heard himself say suddenly.

There was a pause while she thought about it. 'I hope they think so. Haven't you got any family?'

'A half-sister. Perhaps more than one.'

'Don't you know?' she said, laughing. Her face was pretty and animated, even though her hair was untidy and her lipstick chewed. He suspected she was glad to be changing the subject away from the Fleming family and on to his. But he felt her warmth and friendliness, her sheer vitality reached out to move him.

He began to tell her about Letty and then about the astonishing story that there might be another member of the family tucked away in Scotland.

'In Glasgow, of all places.' He shook his head. For such a Londoner, the idea seemed impossible. How could a member of his family have got there? By being born there, Letty had said.

'You ought to go and look.'

'I think my sister has. At least she's dropped out of touch and I suspect that's where she is.' The coffee was beginning to sit strangely on him, she had been wise to leave hers more or less untouched. 'I don't know why I am telling you all this.'

'Because you're a nice man. Kind.'

'Not sure how you can tell.'

With a smile, she said: 'When you've washed a man's shirts and underpants, you do know something about him.'

'I shouldn't have let you do it.'

'It was not for you to say,' said Sarah proudly.

'Now I know you better, Sarah, I think I'd pay you not to do it.'

Soon after that, he left. Peter had still not appeared. Out of all his questions asked in the line of the investigation, perhaps he had not got very much, although he was not so sure about that. But there had certainly been something else. He had a lot to think about.

As he walked home, he reflected that it was almost a love passage. It was not, of course. Just the way it came out.

TEN

COFFIN WENT HOME and let himself into his flat. All was quiet and still, and undusted. Clearly Mrs Brocklebank had not been to clean today. Now he thought about it, she had not been here yesterday either; small chance she would be here tomorrow then, she was avoiding him. He could understand her behaviour. But it would not avail her, he could always go and see her. Would do.

Might be interesting to see the Brocklebank household.

Moodily he put on the kettle for more coffee, powdered this time, he could not rise to the skills performed so effortlessly by Sarah Fleming. Then he decided to make himself an omelette. Should be easy, he decided, you broke the eggs, bashed them around with a fork, not spilling them over yourself if you could help it, then put them in the frying-pan. He had always managed this part with success, but for some reason, he had always found getting the eggs out much harder. As a piece, anyway. They stuck and came out in bits. Black and burnt usually. And if they didn't come out in segments, then the middle fell out as you transferred the pale object to your plate.

He had taken to avoiding putting in a middle. But an omelette empty of content was a sad object. Not nourishing, either. Though by that time, he was not usually thinking of nourishment but the simple satisfaction of hunger.

In a way, he was glad when the doorbell rang commandingly just as he had got the eggs in the pan. He was still hungry, but he was not in trouble.

There was always fish and chips. With a pang, he remembered the last time he had eaten fish and chips, the time he had met Irene Pitt.

The bell rang again, a long, loud peal. He could guess who it was. There was only one person in his life at the moment who rang bells with such commanding force.

'Come in, Paul,' he said, as he opened the door.

'Sorry to barge in.'

The Inspector looked tired. he sniffed. 'Can I smell something burning.'

'Oh damn!' Coffin fled back to the kitchen. In trouble, after all. He shovelled the contents of his frying-pan into the waste-bin and put the pan in the sink. The red-hot handle burnt his hand.

'Turn off the gas,' suggested Lane mildly. He looked at his wounded colleague and did the job himself. 'You have to turn the gas down with eggs.' He had learnt to cook in his first bedsit as a student. 'Of course, a good omelette—that was an omelette?—is very hard to bring off,' he said tactfully.

It was at moments like this that John Coffin realized that the Inspector would go right to the top.

'I can't even bring off a bad one,' he said. 'Come into the sitting-room and have a drink. Do you mind if I eat some bread and cheese?'

The Inspector followed him in, quietly turning off the kettle which had been busy boiling itself dry. Wonder how many frying-pans and kettles he gets through in a week, he mused.

'I don't eat here often,' said Coffin, almost answering his question. 'Not hot food, anyway.'

'Sorry to barge in.'

'Glad to see you.'

'Wait till you hear what I've got to say.'

'Let's have a drink first, then,' said Coffin, pouring out whisky with a generous hand. He didn't drink much himself as a rule and neither did Lane, but tonight was the night for it. Sarah Fleming had unsettled him in more ways than one. Without meaning to, she had let into his mind, like a set of wolves, hard and surprising thoughts about the death of the Pitts. And about herself.

And about himself in relation to her.

'What did you do, then?'

'I know you wanted to speak to Rhoda Brocklebank but I am afraid I've jumped the gun. I've been to see her as well as the other two women. Once I'd seen them, I realized I had to get to her before they did.'

'Go on. I'm interested.'

'They have been tapping the money that Place and Egan left with them for safety. Place left his little pile with his sister, she kept it under the floorboards. William Egan left his with Mrs Brocklebank because he trusted her more than anyone else. He just about could do, because as it turned out she only took a percentage, unlike the other two who got through the lot, but then Egan had more to leave hidden than Place. Roxie Farmer let it all out without much pressure. I think she was glad to confess, and her sister-in-law just said she considered it as much her money as Terry's.'

'She had a point there.'

'It was as much hers as it was Terry's, I suppose, but the Bank he heisted it from might think it had a prior claim. Anyway, they had managed to fend Terry off by pretending the money was hidden in Spain. God help him, he believed it, and he was waiting to get it.'

'Bit of luck for them what happened to him.'

'Oh yes, and they're not expecting him back. Written him off. But Bill Egan was another matter. They were all terrified when they heard he was arriving back prematurely.'

'Must have been a relief when he was killed.'

Lane said: 'I would call their present mood one of relief mixed with fear. They are still frightened.' As if something was hanging over them. 'Especially Rhoda Brocklebank. Once she knew the other two women had talked, it came out like a flood. She kept the money hidden in 22, Church Row so that her husband should not see it.'

'And invented the tale of the house being haunted as a security measure?'

'She thought it advisable, and now of course she more than half believes it herself.'

Coffin sat back. 'Let's run over everything and see what we can put together.' He took a last bite of cheese and biscuit and still looked hungry.

Lane took pity on him. 'Hang on,' he said, and went out to the kitchen. The pan was past rescuing but he thought he could manage something with a non-stick saucepan.

'Don't think I'm doing this out of pity for you,' he called. 'I'm hungry myself.' He looked around the kitchen, tidy but empty, not the sort of kitchen where any serious eating was done. This must make him an ideal employer for Mrs Brocklebank whom he reckoned to be on the lazy side. 'Any more eggs?'

'Box in the refrigerator.'

Coffin sat back. His living-room was one of his rare successes in interior decorating. It had happened by accident, almost, just buying the furniture he liked as he saw it, odd pieces here and there, and then choosing the carpet and curtains in the expensive London store where he had happened to be making inquiries about another crime. The curtains and the carpet was deep yellow and oriental. If anyone spilt anything on it, he would kill them. It was the first time he had loved a carpet, and now he found himself looking at carpets in shop windows.

Paul Lane came back with two plates of scrambled eggs and buttered toast. He had also found time to make some coffee.

Coffin took a mouthful of hot eggs and toast, found it delicious, made a resolve to learn to cook them himself, and started talking.

'About Bill Egan. We know where he was hiding, we know who killed him, although not why it was done with such unnecessary violence.'

'You think that is important?'

'I think it may be, but we may get Place to tell us.' Lane looked doubtful, but Coffin swept on. 'We know what was worrying Rhoda Brocklebank, and Roxie Farmer and Mrs Terry Place. I shall be talking to that trio myself. I don't know what we are going to do about them. Can't just say forgive and forget.'

'If Terry Place recovers he's going to have something to say as well.' Inspector Lane was tidily collecting the plates.

'Is he going to recover?'

Lane shrugged. 'Probably not. He's on a life support system. Kidney failure.'

'I'm glad he spoke up about the shooting on the river before he collapsed again,' said Coffin soberly. 'I must have another word with him. Let me know how things go there.' He thought for a moment, then went on:

'There is a chain of contacts: Egan, Place, Nona, the Pitts.'

'What does that mean?'

'I don't know,' admitted Coffin. 'Perhaps nothing at all. Could be just coincidence. It does happen.' Every policeman knew that. 'Or perhaps Rhoda is right and it is the house. No, I don't accept that. But I do believe that one act of violence seeds another.' He looked out of the window. 'You can forget I said that.'

It wasn't the sort of utterance that the orthodox policeman made in public.

'Which was the original act of violence? We might have to look a long way back.'

Lane was interested but puzzled.

'Wherever it began, it ends in the death of three of the Pitt family by poisoning. And that poison, potassium cyanide. To which the girl Nona might have had access.'

Lane's mouth opened in surprise.

Briskly, Coffin told him of Christopher Court's story and how the MP's tale had led him to investigate the death of Malcolm Kincaid.

'Is that your original act of violence?'

'Could be. There has to be a start somewhere.'

Lane considered. 'All very speculative. We don't know the Pitt girl was there at the scene of his suicide, nor if there was any potassium cyanide left. All we know is that the container or bottle was never found. We'll never know now.'

He had a clear, sceptical and analytical mind, valuable to his boss.

'Have you passed this info along?'

'To Salter? No, not yet. I will, of course, but I don't know what he will make of it.'

Technically, overlooking TAS's watching brief, the investigation into the deaths of the Pitt family was now in the hands of a senior local CID officer, Chief Inspector Chips Salter. He was not an easy man to deal with.

'He's still working on the theory that they were killed by someone from the neighbourhood who resented them and their prosperity.'

Coffin grunted. 'Any evidence?'

'He's floundering,' said Lane. 'But he has one or two family groups lined up. The usual violent, racial outfits who hate anyone not like them. People with a record for interfering with the likes of the Pitts, not ones with their social standing, though.'

'He dislikes me interfering, but I'm going to have to.'

Chief Inspector Chips Salter was one of the officers they had been sent in to bring under control and Salter both guessed this (although all such information was supposed to be highly confidential), and—naturally—resented it.

The remit of the TAS said AID and ASSIST, which meant they had the right to weigh in but the locals had the right to offer obstruction. And did. Trouble had been stitched into the TAS at its inception.

'I shall have to put a report in on him.' Coffin spoke without pleasure.

'He's one of the worst,' said Lane with gloomy satisfaction.

'He always seems a jump ahead of me.' The Chief Inspector appeared to have ready access to their thoughts and plans. 'Didn't he and Jumbo train together?'

Lane nodded. He was no admirer of the casual Chief Inspector Jardine who had been wished on them. 'The same thought occurred to me. Jumbo is a

leaky sieve. Not on purpose, but in the Golf Club...
Those two play together.'

They settled down to a discussion of their problems, and the work they had in front of them. The two young sergeants, Topper and Evans, were assets, Chief Inspector Jardine a known liability. But everyone knew about Jumbo, he was no surprise. He was like an old car that had been around in the neighbourhood for a long time, loaned out among your friends, used and passed on, so that when it got to you in your time, you knew what you were getting.

It was well after midnight before Paul Lane yawned and got up. 'Better get back. The wife will think I've got lost.' It was a joke, she thoroughly understood the demands of his job, it was one of his greatest assets as a policeman. He would never come back home and find she had left an angry note of farewell on the pillow.

Coffin saw him down the staircase and out of the front door, where they stood, still talking.

Paul Lane put his hand in his pocket for his car keys and found something there. He drew it out where it rested on his palm. 'Oh, I remember. Found this at Roxie's. They had a bit of a bonfire in the front garden. This was at my feet and I just picked it up.'

Coffin took it from him. It was a small, two-dimensional, painted cardboard figure of a young woman in flowing mediaeval-style robes. The flat figure stood on a small base as if ready to be moved round a board like a chessman. It was about three inches high.

'Looks like a piece from a game,' said Lane. 'I just hung on to it. You never know.'

'Her,' said Coffin. 'Not it. This is a woman.'

He turned the figurine over. On the back he could just make out some printed words.

TOMBS AND TORTURERS.

And then, horizontally down the spine, so that he had to turn it round to read it in the light of a street lamp.

THE VIRGIN.

'Tombs and torturers?' repeated Lane, after him. 'What does that mean?'

'Think about it,' said Coffin, turning the little figure over in his hand.

It was at this point that he began to realize what a very bizarre and difficult case he had fallen into.

ELEVEN

THE NEXT MORNING Terry Place died in hospital. He had been swinging in and out of consciousness for several days. During this time he had admitted killing William Egan. Unasked, he had admitted the murder several times.

About the motive for killing him Place seemed less clear. Yes, he had feared Bill Egan. He thought Egan would beat him up when they met. Egan had promised to do him this service. He had also engaged to do the same thing for Chief Superintendent John Coffin and one or two other enemies if he could get round to them, but he had let Place know that he had a prior claim.

'So you got in first?'

The questioning was being done by an older detective, Sergeant Jimmy Thackeray, who had known Terry Place well at one time. A transcript of the questions and answers would be sent to all interested parties. All in the TAS would receive one. A senior nurse was also present all the time.

No answer.

After a bit, he said, 'Yes, that would be it.'

'Why did you kill him with such violence, Terry?'

No answer. He never did answer that one.

When he died his wife was by his side, holding his hand. You could hardly say they had been reconciled, but there seemed no rancour between them. Apparently he felt a minimal comfort in contact with her. And after all, she owed him that much.

One other person was present during this period and this was John Coffin. Paul Lane had alerted him to Terry Place's imminent death.

'He's going. But he can still talk. Or just about. If you want to talk to him, you'd better get down there.'

Coffin said: 'Terry, what is this with you and Tombs and Torturers?'

There were other questions he might have asked, such as, What do you know about potassium cyanide? or: Did you have any reason to hate the Pitt family? but somehow this popped out first. For a moment he thought that Terry was going to say something important, because his mouth started to form a word, but nothing came out.

I wish I could guess what it was, thought Coffin. You've never been much help to anyone all your life, but I think you were trying then.

A doctor, young, female, pretty, appeared at this point, and cleared them all out. Mrs Place was allowed to stay.

John Coffin walked away, marvelling at the strangeness of life which made him now mourn a petty criminal whom he had not liked and whom no one had appeared to love, and who might, just possibly, have also poisoned three people. Now he felt a pang at the closeness of life and death. You never knew what you were in for when you got up in the morning.

Before he went to the hospital, John Coffin had had a telephone call from his current girlfriend. She had started a relationship (as she put it) with someone else. So that was over. He found he did not mind. Still, it was part of the day's detritus, to be swept into a tidy heap when he had time. 'You have kept me in the background of your life for too long now; I don't think you will notice when I am not there,' she had said. All too true. Being an actress, she was a girl for the foreground.

In addition, he had called at the Fleming house where he had got no reply to his bell-ringing. Sarah would be at the Polytechnic and the children at school, but what about Peter Fleming? He could be out walking, but Coffin was far from sure. He felt there was a face behind the curtains in the front room that was listening and watching.

If necessary, he would send Sergeant Phyllis Henley, who seemed to understand the ways of the family, to sit outside the door in her car until Peter Fleming either came out or came home.

All this had to be fitted in around the other main tasks of the day. He was an administrator now as well as a detective, so that in the morning he had a report to write, two interviews to conduct, while in the afternoon he must drive to central London to attend a committee. Moreover, although there was no longer any question of any inquiry into the shootings on the river, this was by no means the end of the matter. There was a report to write here, too.

Before the end of the day, he had had a short sharp interview with Chief Inspector Chips Salter, who produced the names of the two families he suspected of killing the Pitts, with his reasons for this suspicion, while at the same time letting John Coffin know he thought he was wasting his time looking elsewhere.

'It's basically a simple matter,' he said, banging his hand on the file of testimony he had produced for inspection. 'And you're letting it get out of hand.'

He managed to convey some contempt for the TAS and its operations at the same time.

'There are these witnesses in the Rosy Crown pub say they heard Tim Cheever say he'd like to clear the Pitts away, and a man who says he heard Flo Coster say, do it with poison. She's a hard one.'

'Just pub talk,' said Coffin.

'Oh, I have confirmation.' Salter was triumphant. 'Two of the Cheever brothers were seen outside the Pitt house the day they died. A witness says she saw them knock on the door.'

'And what do they say they were doing?'

'Selling double glazing.'

'I suppose they do sell it?'

'If they can get any mug to buy it.'

'I don't think you've got enough.'

'Of course it's not enough, but it's a start.'

The trouble with you, my friend, Coffin thought, looking at him, is that you make up your mind first and get the evidence afterwards.

He mustered his own roll-call of suspects: Edward Pitt, Terry Place, possibly the girl, Nona. And you had to consider Christopher Court.

'What about the MP?' he demanded.

'Nothing,' said the Chief Inspector. 'You can't consider him seriously.'

Think so? said Coffin to himself, running over his litany of suspects again in his mind.

Chips Salter was an enormous man, at one time the tallest man in the Force, and he took himself seriously. He went on tartly, scenting the unspoken criticism:

'It's a start,' he repeated with every appearance of obstinacy. 'I'm getting a case together and it's going in the right direction. I know these families.' And you don't, was the implication. 'They both belong to the National Front and they both were in that tarring and feathering riot down Deptford High Street. One of my men had to have plastic surgery after that little lark. I didn't get them for that effort.'

So now he would get them for something they might not have done. He had not got a result on the first case because he had not been sharp enough. So sloppy police work would be followed by further sloppy police work.

'What about the Costers?'

'More dicey there,' admitted Salter. 'But they would be the source of the poison. Rupert Coster is a porter in a wholesale jewellery firm. They use potassium cyanide commercially. He might have access to the poison.'

He had it all worked out, but Coffin did not believe a word of it.

'Might have access?' he inquired.

'I'm working on it.' Chief Inspector Salter gathered his papers together and stood up.

He disliked the TAS intensely, knew very well he was an object of study for them, knew (through the indiscretions of his old friend Jumbo Jardine) how they were going about it, and meant to defend himself stoutly.

Attack was the best method of defence.

'I'll get my evidence before you get yours,' he said.

Did he bang the door? He decided to be subtle and closed it very slowly and carefully.

Coffin sat back in his chair and laughed.

Last laugh of the day.

HE HADN'T FORGOTTEN Rhoda Brocklebank and his need to talk to her, but he was saving her up. Her time would come, but he had to choose that time. He did not want to bring her in to talk to him, nor did he want to interview her in the presence of her devoted but sharp-eyed husband.

Before he went home that evening, he managed to consult Sergeant Phyllis Henley. He came across her having a cup of tea and a chocolate biscuit in the canteen.

She looked up in surprise; she swallowed her mouthful of chocolate digestive, and tried to stand up.

'Don't get up, Phyllis.' He sat down beside her.

'Let me get you a cup, Chief Inspector.'

He allowed her to walk across to the counter for a cup of tea because he felt she was flustered, not an emotion one easily associated with Sergeant Henley, and it might settle her down.

'I was having a chocolate biscuit to celebrate,' she admitted, when she was sitting down again. 'Don't usually indulge.'

'What are you celebrating?' He wondered if he ought to know. Promotion? Something to do with her husband? He knew she was married.

'I've written an article on Women in the Force, and it's going to be published. The editor just rang up, asking for pictures. Do you think I'll be allowed to use them?'

'Don't see why not. What's it for?'

'*Woman Today*. They are having a series on professional women at work. I'm one. I'm ever so chuffed.'

'Congratulations. Well done.'

She smiled modestly, and took another bite of chocolate biscuit. A crumb of chocolate stuck to her lip, where Coffin watched it slowly melt as he spoke to her.

'I want to talk to Rhoda Brocklebank and Peter Fleming, but I can't seem to get at them. Can you help?'

Phyllis set down her cup. She did not ask him why he wanted to speak to them. No need. She had her own sources of information. 'About Mrs Brocklebank, I don't think I can do much there. About Peter Fleming, I saw him walking down Romney Road as I came here.' She had a motorcycle herself on which she sped down the roads. 'And that's his usual way home. He'll be there now, I'd say. Sarah will be back to get him his tea. He won't miss that.'

'Thanks. I'll get along.'

'Can't help you about the lady, though.'

He stood up. 'Well, if you think of anything.'

'Wait a minute... I've seen her going along to the library regularly, pretty well every night. She must be quite a reader. I should think you could find her there.'

'Thanks again.' He felt doubtful about patrolling the library precincts to accost Mrs Brocklebank on her way to collect an armful of romance.

The sergeant had not finished. 'And then after that, she pops into the Red Trafalgar.' The Red Trafalgar was the public house called the Trafalgar Arms with its exterior painted in bright red as opposed to the Green Trafalgar, a pub of the same name, over Deptford Bridge and painted a dark green. 'Not always,' went on the sergeant, 'but often.'

'Thank you. You've given me a lot.' He knew he had come to the right person. She must go round the district like one of those fishes with a kind of fishing net in their jaws, sucking up all the information as they did the little fish. All the same, he liked her; she was a woman of great strength. 'See if you can get a word with Rhoda Brocklebank.'

'Wouldn't it be easier for you?'

'No, I want to concentrate on the boy, Peter. I think you might get more out of her. Woman to woman, you know.' The sergeant looked doubtful, but gave a nod.

'Get her to talk about the girl, Nona Pitt, and about Terry Place.'

Phyllis was surprised. 'Place? Do you suspect him of being involved in the Pitt poisoning.'

'He's always been in my mind.'

He carried with him a memory of the perplexed, thoughtful look on her face.

With the information she had given him, he approached the Fleming house in Queen Charlotte's Alley in the hope of seeing Peter on his own without the disturbing presence of Sarah.

The boy himself opened the door. He looked taken aback to see the policeman.

'I thought you were Sal forgotten her key. She often does. Is it about your washing?' He stared around vaguely. 'I don't know where it is. Could you come back later when Sal is here?'

'It's you I want to see.'

He was inside by then, having quietly inserted himself while he was talking.

The boy stood where he was, not welcoming, not unwelcoming either, but neutral.

'How are you?'

'I'm all right,' Peter said briefly. 'So what is it? I'm not sure I want to talk.'

'I do have to ask some questions. I left it as long as I could.'

'Well, you aren't the first. Another one of you came round. Two in fact. Came together. A big bald man and a little one with a red face.'

Without any difficulty Coffin identified Chief Inspector Salter and one of his inspectors, a man called Stoker, said to have his eye on the main chance. He too was about to figure in Coffin's confidential TAS report.

'They wanted to ask questions about Nona Pitt. Did she have any boyfriends round here. Had there been any trouble.'

'What sort of trouble?'

Peter gave the shrug that Coffin began to recognize as a family gesture. 'I don't know. Fights, jealousy, that sort of thing. That's what he seemed to mean.'

'And had there been?'

Again a shrug, this time dismissive. 'No, not that I know. Nona wasn't like that. She was private. Quiet. You had to get to know her.'

'She was a strikingly pretty girl, though.'

'I suppose she was.'

'I know she was. You were in love with her, weren't you? Surely it was her looks that attracted you.'

'Nona was only a kid when I first knew her. She didn't turn into what you saw till she came back from New York.'

'But you were friends even in those early days?'

'She followed me around.'

'And when she came back the situation was reversed? You followed her?'

'We were still friends,' he said quickly. 'We'd both grown up a bit, that's all. Nona'd grown up a lot in New York.'

'And where does Terry Place come in?'

He was sniffing round, trying to build up a picture of the relationship. He was sure there was something.

'Terry hadn't met her.' The response came at once.

'They met in the tunnel.'

'Well, yes, there.'

'Why did you take Nona there?'

'We were sightseeing. I was showing her places of interest. She liked historical places.' It was pat, could be true.

'The tunnel was no place of beauty.'

'But interesting. That was all.'

Coffin nodded. 'And you did not know Terry Place was there?'

'No.'

'Your sister thinks you did.'

He shook his head. 'Don't take any notice of Sarah. She doesn't know anything about it. How could she?'

Coffin did not answer. How could she? It was something she had felt rather than known logically. She had implied as much.

All this time they had been standing by the front door. He closed it. 'Can we sit down?'

He did not wait for an answer but led the way through to the kitchen. Peter had been sitting at the table on which there was a mug of tea and a brightly coloured magazine.

'Sit down, Peter. I didn't mean to interrupt your tea. Carry on drinking.'

'It's cold now.' He swept the magazine into a drawer, then carried the tea mug over to the sink where he emptied it. He leant against the sink and turned to face Coffin. 'Take a chair.'

'Thanks. Your sister says there was some game you played with Terry Place. What was it?'

'I don't know what Sarah thinks she's up to.'

'And you didn't play any game with Terry?'

'We were both interested in things like the *Cutty Sark,* and the old tunnel and old Greenwich. Terry wasn't educated, but he was interested in old things.'

'So it wasn't a game, just a common interest?'

'Yes, that's it.'

'Not at work at the moment, are you?'

'No, but I'm going back tomorrow.'

That will stop you walking round the streets and put you where I can find you, thought Coffin.

'Does the name Malcolm Kincaid mean anything to you?'

Peter frowned. 'Yeah. I do seem to remember the name.'

'Remember anything about him.'

'No. Should I?'

'Nona ever talk about him?'

'Nona? Not to me. Was he a boyfriend? In New York?' He shook his head. 'I wouldn't know in that case.'

'Nothing to do with New York.'

Coffin stood up to leave. He thought he had got all he could for the time being. At the very least, he was beginning to form a picture of the relationship between Peter Fleming, Nona Pitt and Terry Place. In some ways it hardly seemed to exist; in another way, it had almost brought about the death of all three. As it was, Peter was the only survivor. And yet it might be pointless to speculate on it. It could be like the mysterious caller on the telephone to Mr Wallace requesting the visit to Qualtrough Avenue: you just did not know if it existed at all. Or like, the note from a sick friend sent to the about-to-be-murdered Mrs Abby Borden of Fall River: it might mean something or might mean nothing at all.

But for himself he disliked coincidence of any sort and always sought for a logical answer. Even in cases in the past, where he had looked for one and found none, he had always felt if he had searched harder or been luckier, then the answer would have been found. Like the case, some years ago, when two men died in the same way from similar stab wounds on the same day and in the same street. He never was able to prove a connection, but he remained convinced that there must have been one. The woman convicted of killing one man always denied killing or even knowing the other.

He glanced around the kitchen. Unlike yesterday it was untidy, with children's clothes littering the chairs, a doll which must belong to Weenie on the floor and unwashed dishes in the sink.

Peter saw him looking. 'My day for clearing up, Sal's day at the Poly. I ought to get started.' He began to tidy the muddle, moving with the same economic efficiency his sister had shown. The brother and sister had a lot more in common than was at first apparent.

'I ought to collect the little 'uns from their minder, too.'

'Sarah's out all day?'

'Yes, we have turns.' He was taking a dish out of the refrigerator. 'Shan't see her for hours. She leaves a supper for me to cook.' He was running water over the dishes in the sink, swilling them round rapidly and then placing them on the side. 'That's it, eh? I'll have to get on with this.'

Coffin thought the boy was glad to have an excuse to close the interview. He moved a pace, as if to go.

'Efficient girl, your sister.'

'Oh yes, Sal's pretty good.'

'It must be hard on her taking on all this responsibility.' He picked up a toy and placed it with the others on the pile. 'Especially with the children.'

'Sometimes she says she'll take the kids out to the middle of a lake and drop them in. I don't think she'd do it, but you can never be sure with Sal.'

Coffin gave him a long look and he wasn't laughing.

'How do you get on with her?' he asked drily.

'Oh, fine, but I'm a bit big to drop in a lake.' Now he was smiling.

At the door, Peter said: 'She didn't like Nona. Didn't really like the Pitts. She may say she did, but she didn't.'

He saw Coffin to the door politely, holding the door open.

Coffin went away to his own home, feeling miserable and puzzled.

He wasn't sure he enjoyed what he was turning up.

Peter had made an attack on his sister. He had not accused her of killing the Pitts, but he had certainly hinted that she was capable of it.

He turned round at the corner of Queen Charlotte's Alley to look back. Peter was still at the front door, staring at him.

It seemed inevitable after this that he should take himself to the nearest fish and chip shop to eat his supper. There were a series of small booths in which you could crouch to eat. It was necessary to do this since the roof was both low and decorated with swags of imitation seaweed; a tall man was at a disadvantage.

He ordered his meal of cod and chips and no vinegar, then sat down to await its arrival. No one knew him there, which was just as well. It was not the thing for a high-ranking police officer with still rising ambition to be eating his supper in Jack's Fish Bar. At his age and with his rank, he was supposed to have a happy home life with a cheerful wife and two children, both enjoying higher education. He seemed to have missed all that somehow. His ex-girlfriend was no more of a cook or a home-maker than he was. Her speciality was a kind of uncooked avocado mousse that was better avoided, although her martinis were good. She was a celebrated actress whom he had known and loved, on and off, almost since her first appearance on the stage. They had drifted into a brief alliance now because she was out of work and he was at a loose end emotionally, but it had not worked. It never would, she was too sophisticated for him, and he was too clever for her.

The cod arrived, and was enjoyable. The place was almost empty except for an old man in one corner and a boy and a girl eating chicken and chips two booths away. He was too late or too early for the main trade.

'Like some tomato sauce, dear?' The waitress leaned across the counter.

'No, thank you.'

'Brown sauce? Bread and butter?' She was bored, longing to talk to someone. After an evening of work here, she felt she must look like a cod or haddock herself with dull eyes and open mouth. Frozen too. They all came frozen, in packs ready to cook. Two nights a week she worked here and then on the third night she washed her hair and all her clothes to get rid of the smell of fried fish and went dancing. The other four nights she stayed at home, studying, since she was a student at the same Polytechnic that was educating Sarah Fleming and Sergeant Jones's son, but she knew neither of them as she was a year older and taking different subjects.

She could tell she was going to get no response from Coffin, although he was being polite, when a crowd of youngsters swarmed in from the local youth club. Gratefully, she went across to take their order. On the way, she put an evening paper on the table for Coffin. Let him amuse himself. 'Here you are,' she said kindly. She dropped the dear, she had made a mistake there, he was not the sort you called dear. She knew how to adapt her manner. She was studying anthropology, and was the first member of her family to enter higher education.

Coffin sat eating and reading. He could hear snatches of conversation from across the room. They seemed to be talking about a pop star called Sid Vicious.

In the newspaper the headlines were still speculating about a General Election and Mr Callaghan was once again promising to make an early statement. The Election had been on and off for weeks now. He knew where his vote would go, expected no good to come of it and wasn't worried. He had long since gone dead on politicians. He turned the pages. Films, theatre. A play about Elvis Presley had opened, and *Sleuth* was still running. And yes, here was a preview of Stella Pinero's new play. Praise for her performance, critical reserve about the play, the welcome suggestion it would run and run. Good. Stella needed a solid commercial success. She wouldn't like that photograph of herself, however.

He sighed and turned a page. He was into the crime page now. The usual run of mugging, housebreaking and shoplifting. What he summed up as amateur crime. None the less nasty, some of the cases, for all that. One major bank robbery had just come to trial. He cast a professional eye over the report. A bungled job, the gang deserved to go down. Reading the judge's summing up, they were obviously about to do so.

In America a lady had been sentenced to death for hiring an assassin to shoot her father and her step-father.

At the bottom of the page, one case had a wide spread to itself. A strange picture as well.

EXECUTIONER'S AXE USED IN SLAYING, ran the headline in heavy print.

There was a drawing of an axe with a hooded figure swinging the weapon over his head. The figure was markedly masculine, with all sexual characteristics stressed.

He sat back. The effect produced was unpleasant, nasty.

A young man, eighteen years old, a student at Essex University, had cut off the head of one of his teachers, accusing him of handing out unfairly poor marks. He had then lain in wait for the man's wife and daughter and knifed them to death as they returned from a shopping trip. He had cut off the girl's head and put it next to her father's on the garden path, where they had been found by a neighbour. The so-called Executioner's Axe was really a woodman's axe on a long handle. He had been a bright student, but his work had deteriorated over the past year, and he had thoroughly deserved his poor marks.

'Bring me a cup of tea, dear,' said Coffin to the waitress as she passed, absently reproducing her own tones. She gave him a surprised look, but did so.

'Tea, sir,' she said. 'Sugar is on the table.' The tea was heavily milked and pale brown in a thick white cup. Coffin drank thirstily, and read on.

The student's friends said he was 'wacky' and 'into violence', but until his murderous frenzy they had believed it to be entirely in his mind. A verbal game, showing, they had thought, its only physical manifestation in certain tattoos of dragons and executioners on his arms.

'Now we know it was not,' his best friend had said. His girlfriend said she had loved him.

He had tried to kill himself before being arrested. His mother said he had been a 'normal boy'. He had lost his father through an industrial accident the year before he went to university. She blamed his breakdown on the university, where he had become 'a different boy'. His mother spoke as if she believed an unnatural weight of learning had fallen on her son's head and knocked him into madness.

His girlfriend, a fellow student, said he was normal about sex, but they 'hadn't done much'. Reading between the lines, Coffin sensed she felt lucky to be alive.

He drank his tea, paid his bill, left a good tip and walked home. He took the evening paper with him.

Back in his flat, he read the news item again. He considered whom he knew in the Essex CID and whom he could tap for information.

He dialled Paul Lane's home number. To his surprise the Inspector answered himself.

'Sorry to break into your evening at home.' He could hear the sound of music in the background. Mozart, he thought. 'Just a query. Didn't Ben Horridge go to Essex?'

'Yes, transferred for family reasons. So he said. Think he really got fed up with where he lived. His wife came from that way. Near Braintree, I think.'

'Do you have his number?'

There was a silence for a moment. Then: 'Might dig it out. Give me a minute. I'll call you back.'

'Thanks, Paul. Do the same for you one day.'

While he waited, Coffin went to the window to look out. A smart car was moving down the road. Something familiar struck him. He moved his head to get a better look at the driver.

It was the MP, Christopher Court.

Now what's he doing here?

The telephone broke into his thoughts with Paul Lane triumphantly coming through with the Essex number.

'Why do you want it?'

'Just something I'm checking.'

Lane accepted it without comment, although at another time he might have pressed for more of an answer; he wasn't a man who liked to be kept in the dark. But there was laughter, and there were children's voices in the background as well as music. Coffin sensed the other man wanted to be quietly at home with his family tonight.

He stood by the telephone, his hand ready to dial the number in Essex. He should have been like that, happy with a wife and children. It hadn't worked that way. Not that he hadn't tried, perhaps he had tried too often.

Instead, he was alone with what could be the beginning of a collection of oriental carpets, and pining, however slightly, for a young girl one-half his age.

He dialled Essex and, the gods relenting, got through at once to the man he wanted.

'Ben? John Coffin speaking.'

Silence for a moment, and then a surprised voice said: 'Oh yes. You're a kind of Supremo now, aren't you? What can I do for you?'

'I wanted some information about a local case of yours. It might just be of help to me. The student who killed his tutor and then cut off his head.'

'Oh, that one. Daniel Moore. Killed more than his professor. Did in the wife and the daughter as well.'

'I suppose he's mad?'

'Well, I don't know about that. Not normal, but not certifiable. Or so the medics say.'

'I've got a case here that worries me, and I wondered if there were any parallels.'

'Not my case,' said Horridge cautiously. 'I've been busy mopping up a crowd of drug smugglers.'

Coffin ignored this precautionary retreat. 'Did he give any warning this could happen? Anything significant?'

'I heard a tale that he and a couple of friends used to meet and act out stories.'

'Amateur dramatics, you mean?'

'I suppose you could call it that. Pretty violent tales by all accounts. But I don't know how much truth there is in it. Been lots of stories going round, as you can imagine.'

'A kind of club?' asked Coffin.

'Don't know about that.' He paused, then said: 'What hasn't got in the papers is another case like it. Six months ago. Involved a girl, this time. She killed her mother with an axe. Said mother had been marked for termination.'

'Did they know each other, Daniel Moore and the girl. What was her name?'

'No evidence. She was Evelyn Bond.'

'Did they correspond?'

'No evidence.'

'And she didn't go in for violent amateur dramatics with a bunch of friends?'

Horridge laughed. 'Not that I heard, but I believe it was looked into.'

'She didn't play any sort of game?' Coffin said hopefully. He did not want to provide the name: Tombs and Torturers. He was not quite sure how far he could trust Horridge. Besides, he was beginning to guess that there might be other games, and if so, he would like to know.

'Not that I know of.'

'Did the girl say anything herself?'

'Suicide. She poisoned herself.'

Then he added: 'She had her head on a pile of paper comics. Nasty imports. Very full of violence. She may have got the idea from them. So may Moore, because he had them too.'

'Can you give me her details? Address, dates?'

'Don't quote me.' But he went away to look and dates and the address of Evelyn Bond were provided. She had come from across the county in Southend.

They talked for a while longer before Coffin put down the receiver and returned to look out of the window.

He could not see where Terry Place and his killing of William Egan, nor the idea that he might have been a poisoner, fitted into all this, perhaps nowhere, but his violence seemed to have a kind of parallel in the Essex cases, which might illuminate his own problem.

Once again he telephoned Lane. This time he could almost hear a patient sigh coming down the telephone.

'Tomorrow I want you to send young Evans down to Essex.' He quickly ran over the story of the Essex murders. 'Here are the names and addresses.' He waited while the Inspector got them down. 'I want all the background detail he can get. And tell Evans to be as quiet as possible about it.'

He felt more cheerful as he pottered about the flat. He could feel ideas moving in his mind and he knew that was a good sign.

A block was going to shift. He wondered what Phyllis Henley had got from Rhoda Brocklebank.

He put the television on to watch a news programme, but before it had started, the telephone at his elbow rang.

It was Phyllis Henley herself. She was not a woman to sound excited, but he picked up a thread of something like it in her voice.

'Sir, could I come round to have a talk? I've got on to something.' She was speaking from a call-box, he could hear the noises of the road, traffic, an aeroplane passing overhead. 'No, not Rhoda Brocklebank, although I have seen her, in fact she has helped. This is something else.'

'Come round,' Coffin said.

'I've just got one more thing I want to do. Be seeing you.'

And she was gone; she sounded triumphant.

He watched some television, then sat back to read a book about oriental carpets. He was interested, but the room was warm and he was tired; soon his eyelids drooped.

When he woke up, stiff and uncomfortable, the early summer dawn was lighting the room.

He moved, turning off his reading lamp and yawning.

Phyllis Henley had not turned up. Probably she had been kept late by whatever it was she was doing and had decided to leave it until the morning.

Still yawning, he made himself a cup of tea and took it to bed. He was asleep within two minutes.

Outside in the road, a cat yowled.

TWELVE

FOR THE FIRST HOUR of that morning, from eight until nine, Coffin worked at home, drinking tea and making forays to the telephone. He had discovered how to make reasonable toast. You simply stood by the grill and never took your eyes off it until it was the colour you wanted. The trick was to keep watching. Remove your gaze for a second and the whole process got away with you. He had charred a good many slices of bread and sent several up in flames before he discovered this simple device.

He was in a good mood, it looked like being one of those easy days. You could always tell. For instance, he didn't burn the toast.

With tea and toast and telephone calls he was busy. He rang Inspector Lane to check that Sergeant Evans had been sent off on the business in Essex, to be told Evans was already on his way there.

Before shaving, he rang his office and spoke to the woman police constable who acted as his secretary. She told him what calls he had received and what was waiting in the post.

'Any message from Sergeant Henley?'

'No, sir.' Then she remembered something. 'Wait a bit, there was a call from her husband. But he wouldn't leave a message.'

People could be very tiresome like that, he thought.

He tried several times to talk to his sister Laetitia on the telephone, but she continued to be elusive. He had no doubt she was in Scotland. It was time she surfaced and told him what she was up to.

He had a bath and shave and spoke to his secretary again. She relayed several more messages, conveying by her voice that she thought it was time he appeared in his office. She was a careful, punctilious girl but one who did not like responsibility, not even the responsibility of knowing when and how to lie for her superior. But she was clever, Coffin thought her very clever, and he was training her.

Chief Inspector Salter was anxious to see him and she had made an appointment for him to see the Chief Superintendent later that day. She hoped it was all right?

'You've got my diary, Jean. If the time is clear, then he can come in.'

He wondered what Salter wanted. He knew by now that Salter had plenty of sins both of omission and commission on his conscience and he felt no compunction in letting him worry.

'No message from Sergeant Henley?'

'No, sir. But I saw her husband crossing the car park.' James Henley worked in Records. 'She must be around. Her bike's there. Been there all the morning.'

'Well, try and get hold of her. Tell her to get in touch with me.'

'Yes, sir.'

His secretary's voice was bright and cheerful. Give her a direct order and she knew where she was. She was also marvellously quick in carrying out what was asked of her. Coffin thought she would have made a marvellous soldier.

He went back to his worktable at home in Church Row, confident that Sergeant Phyllis Henley would soon be captured by Jean and brought to him.

He had several files of paper in front of him. There were some reports so confidential that even Jean might not see them; they were better kept at home. In the wall he had a specially constructed safe, for the installing of which official funds had been provided. Not even Paul Lane knew of its existence, although he was clever enough to have guessed it might be there.

Jean rang back in about an hour. 'Sorry I haven't been able to get Sergeant Henley for you. She seems to have covered her tracks with skill. But her bike's still there.'

'Have you telephoned her home?'

'Yes, no answer.'

'What about her husband?'

'He came in and went out again.' Jean added: 'Someone said it was their married daughter's birthday, so perhaps that's it.' It was like Jean to think of a happy family reason for a slight disappearance. Drink, a quarrel or even illness would always come second with her.

'Keep on trying.'

'I expect she'll get in touch with you herself, sir.'

Yes, Phyllis Henley, the tough professional, would tell him when she had hard information, so he could only conclude she was still working on her lead. He had already summed her up as someone who hated to admit defeat. Paul Lane had warned him that Phyllis liked to play things her own way, and now it looked as though she did indeed.

He wished she'd surface. He hated playing guessing games.

Dust was beginning to deposit itself over his furniture, while the kitchen floor needed scrubbing where he had dropped an egg on it. A visit from Mrs Brocklebank was long overdue. He wondered if she had abandoned him for ever.

He hoped she would be back. In a strange kind of way, they suited each other. There was a link, too. She had brought Sarah Fleming into his life, which was something he could not forget.

In the late morning he left the house to walk down Church Row to the garage where he kept his car. He had a meeting to attend in London.

The day had been hot and sunny, bringing out the flies. There seemed more around than usual. One great bluebottle circled his head, ignoring his efforts to brush it away.

He liked the heat of the sun on his back, but somehow the day no longer felt right. It was not going to be such an easy day, after all.

He strolled down the road, thinking, and not for the first time, what a remarkably quiet and empty road

Church Row was. It was in bright sunlight on one side and in deep shadow on the other.

As he got nearer to No. 22 he decided that Mrs Brocklebank had been neglecting her duties here as well.

That famous stain was back on the front steps. Something must have got spilt on them. As he got closer he saw that there was a series of red drops with the characteristic trailing pear shape as of blood which had dripped from a wound. Or a knife.

A patch of flies had been attracted. As he got closer still to the house the fly above his head left him to rejoin its fellows.

The Chief Superintendent walked towards the house. He had seen flies behave like that before. Once in a dirty butcher's shop in Hackney and once in another scene of butchery.

The stains on the step did look remarkably like blood. Mrs Brocklebank, had she been here, would no doubt have pointed them out with triumph. 'Told you so,' she could have said.

He tried the front door. Locked.

Looking down the basement steps which led to a paved area from which a door led straight into that kitchen which had secretly housed Bill Egan, he thought he could see that the door was ajar.

Slowly he walked down the steps. The door stood open a few inches. He pushed it back against some pressure from inside. He put his head round the door.

'Rhoda?' he called questioningly. 'Mrs Brocklebank. You there?' He took a step into the kitchen.

Then he stopped, drawing in his breath sharply.

Sergeant Phyllis Henley lay on her side with her head on her hands. The key which she must have been holding had fallen beside her.

She had her head on her hands, but neither was attached to her body. They were about a foot apart by themselves, and lying in a pool of blood.

SHE WAS COLD, she had been dead some time. After he checked this, he stepped carefully back, touching nothing. The necessary telephone calls would have to be made from his own flat.

He closed the door and walked up the steps. Mrs Brocklebank is right about this house, after all, he thought. It is a bloody house.

THIRTEEN

'SHE DIDN'T DIE easily,' said the police surgeon to John Coffin. He was kneeling by the body, examining its wounds. He was an elderly Scotsman, a man of the north, who had worked all his life in South London and was now near to retirement; he had known Phyllis Henley for almost all of her career. Her work with children and women had brought them together often. He did not like his present task.

'She wouldn't; she was a professional. A tough police officer.'

'She put up a fight.'

Dr McIntyre's examination had been a necessary, first, brief run-over, made without disturbing the body too much. Photographs, measurements, plans of the room would all be done in due course, each in its appointed order. The drill was well worked out and always the same, used for every murder. Special feeling would go into it now. This was the murder of a police officer, one of their own, no one would step aside.

Coffin did not look at the severed hands, where he imagined the signs of a fight would show.

But the doctor did not spare him. 'Look at the left hand.'

Coffin looked. He saw a deep incised wound across the angle of the thumb and the first finger, with another cut on the fleshy mound of the thumb. There were further cuts across the fingers where they flexed.

'Typical defence wounds,' said McIntrye. 'She was gripping the knife to ward off the attack.'

'He came at her from the front then?'

'Meebe, I haven't made up my mind. She has a stab in the back and the look of a woman surprised.'

Coffin did not answer. He let Mac have his Celtic whims, everyone did; he was vastly experienced and had been right so often.

'Now look you here.'

The doctor had rolled up the dead woman's sleeves to examine her arms. She had been wearing a light cotton shirt with a dark blue skirt. On the upper arms were bruises and abrasions. There was no bleeding, the contusions were subcutaneous, the skin had been protected by her shirt.

'Those bruises were caused by her assailant gripping her arms during the attack.'

'The killer must be marked too,' said Coffin.

'I should hope so.' McIntyre pointed to the right hand. 'There are cuts and bruises on the wrist and knuckles. There will be skin and blood under the nails. From the murderer. With any luck that will give you some help.'

'If we know where to look.'

'I shall be hoping you will soon,' said the doctor severely. 'She was a good lass and deserved better than this.'

All around them was, once again in this terrible house, intense police activity. It was only recently that a police presence had been withdrawn from No. 22 after the Pitt deaths. Several rooms, including the dining-room and library, were still sealed.

Now they were all back again, a Scene of Crime officer, a civilian this time, one whom Coffin did not know, the police photographer waiting to start his work, and a CID Inspector from the local police. A new team, in the old house, with a fresh crime.

The doctor and Chief Superintendent Coffin stood aside as the photographer moved in to start his unenviable task of recording the remains. He too had known Phyllis Henley. Their last work together had been with a dead child. He had not enjoyed that photo session either, but he disliked this even more.

Did it make it worse when you knew the victim? When you had worked side by side? And he had to answer: Yes, it did.

'How did she die?'

Even as he asked it, Coffin thought it was a monstrous question to pose.

Phyllis Henley was so obviously, terribly dead. But for professional reasons, he had to know the exact cause of death. There would be a report to write. One of the many reports that would be written. A report from the Scene of Crime officer, one from the police surgeon, another from the police pathologist, and a whole clutch, probably, from the numerous forensic scientists who would be involved. A lot of different disciplines were going to be dragged in.

'Let the clever pathology chaps in their laboratory decide that,' said Dr McIntyre. 'She had a deep stab in the back, but to my mind that's not the one that killed her. I mark the stab in the abdomen as the most likely one. But we'll see.'

'I expect you're right.'

'Likely. But we'll bow to the experts.' He never did, of course, and would fight for his own answer doggedly. Only he rarely had to; he had an eye; it was respected.

'And how long has she been dead?'

'Ach now, that's harder. As you very well know, my lad.'

'Make a guess.'

'The pathologist will be here soon. Let's leave it to him.'

'You were here first.'

'There are so many variables.' McIntyre shrugged. 'It's been a hot night, with not much draught down here. She's well clothed. I'd like to make a body puncture and wait, till I committed myself.'

'Come on, Mac. Why do you always make difficulties?'

'Rigor is passing away.'

'I noticed that when you moved her arm.'

Already it was easier to talk about Phyllis Henley as a body.

'So I suppose death could have taken place about twelve hours ago.' Hastily he added: 'Give or take a bit. It could be an hour or so longer.'

Coffin nodded. 'Thanks.'

It was now after midday. Sergeant Henley had spoken to him about ten-thirty last night. She could have been killed not long afterwards.

'Is there anything else you've noticed?'

Dr McIntyre shrugged. 'Nothing you won't see for yourself. You've observed the key?'

The key to the basement door of No. 22, which had rested by Phyllis Henley's dead hands.

'I have.' And asked himself how she came by it. 'Wonder where she got it?'

'That's your business, not mine.' Dr McIntyre was slowly removing his rubber gloves. He had done all he could, he would make his report, and Phyllis Henley's body would become someone else's study.

'What did you mean by her being surprised?'

'Just that. She may have felt safe here, been surprised to have been attacked. Or her attacker may have been someone she did not expect. It's just my impression, you know. Ignore it.'

'I'll think about it. Thanks for mentioning it. Might be important.'

Dr McIntyre was packing up his bags. He always brought two, ancient black leather bags that had seen long service, into which he packed with great method all the gloves, tweezers, thermometers and rulers that long usage had shown him he needed. These bags were known in the district as Mac's Packs. Out of one of them he drew a small notebook, in which he proceeded to write.

'My expenses.'

But Coffin knew it was much more than that. He was said to keep a tally, an account of all his cases. In its way, this was a famous book.

'Going to write a book, Mac?' It was the traditional joke, someone always made it, it might as well be him now, although laughter was far from both of them.

'Mebbe, mebbe not. But this is an entry I would have been glad not to put down.'

Coffin heard feet coming down the staircase from the upper floor of the house. He recognized the voices of the local CID inspector and of the Home Office pathologist.

'I'll be off,' said McIntyre hastily, making for the outer stairs to the street from the basement. 'Say my by-bys for me.' Between him and the famous pathologist now arriving, there was no love lost.

Coffin stayed on, spoke briefly to the two men, who were polite but not cordial, and departed in his turn.

He telephoned Jean, who already knew the news, and had cancelled several of his local appointments, including the one with Chief Inspector Salter who had been 'so anxious to see him' and who was probably even more anxious now, and told her he was preparing to leave for London and his meeting. Life had to go on.

He had a brief thought for Sergeant Evans now in Essex, collating cases of bloody murders connected with fantasy games. 'Any call from Essex?' he asked.

'None, sir.'

In the brief walk from No. 22 to his own flat he had pulled from the back of his mind a conviction that had been forming there without much conscious thought on his part, just something he knew.

He washed thoroughly, standing under his shower while the hot water poured over him. Nothing could wash away the beastliness of that house or the horror of the sight of Phyllis Henley's body, but he felt the need to try.

He was dirty, guilty, guilty as hell. It was his fault she had died. No matter that it had been police business, and that someone had to do it, he had personally selected Phyllis Henley yesterday. Chosen her as she sat drinking tea and eating chocolate biscuits and enjoying her small triumph.

He had never hated himself more.

When he was dressed, in a clean shirt and a fresh suit, he telephoned Inspector Lane.

He plunged straight in, not bothering to enter into any explanations, knowing that Paul Lane would be thoroughly informed of the death of Sergeant Henley. News like that travelled.

'Paul? Get hold of Topper and send him round to Rhoda Brocklebank. If he can't find her at home, tell him to look in the public library in the afternoon. If that's no good, he's to try the Red Trafalgar when it opens. She ought to be in one or the other. Then he's to get her to admit that she gave Phyllis Henley the key to No. 22. I'm sure that's where Phyllis got it from. He's to get a statement about their meeting. Tell him that.'

'Right.' Lane was short, sounding angry.

Paul Lane's almost silent acceptance of the message told Coffin, if he had not known before, how deeply everyone felt the murder of Sergeant Henley.

When Coffin returned from central London late that night, he looked in at the TAS office. Lane was still there, hunched over his desk. He muttered a greeting.

Coffin turned over the papers and messages that Jean had left on his own desk. Nothing from Evans, who might still be in Essex. 'Did Topper talk to Rhoda Brocklebank?'

'Yes. And she did give the key to Phyllis. Claims she asked for it.'

'What else? She must have had something to say about their interview.'

'She says the sergeant just asked her questions about Nona Pitt, and then about Terry Place.'

Probing, Coffin thought. Following instructions doing what I asked. He felt more guilty than ever.

'Phyllis leave any record of the conversation?'

'She probably left notes. She may not have had time.'

'She telephoned me from a public call-box somewhere. It may have been the Red Trafalgar.'

She would have sat there writing her notes. He didn't think so, though. Where had Phyllis gone, in between leaving Mrs Brocklebank and telephoning him? It might explain why she had gone to No. 22 later that night.

'If her notebook was on her body, then you will be able to see it when forensics have finished with it.'

'Yes.' He could see delays and frustrations here. Salter would not be cooperative and would have passed the word down the line: Don't be over-eager to help the bastards in TAS.

And here on his desk, just under his hand, was another message from Jean to bear out this thought: Chief Inspector Salter is very anxious to see you.

When Coffin got back to his own flat, all he found there in the way of post was an enigmatic postcard from his sister Laetitia: she had sent him a view of Edinburgh from the air, with a message scribbled on the back: I am going to the law. With love from Letty.

It was incomprehensible, and, he thought, a little alarming. What did she mean?

'Damn,' said Coffin and went to bed. Not a good day, one of the worst.

He was a man who had started out in his career simple and full of hope, but his life had been so marked by violent and terrible happenings that his character was now seamed and rocky like a mountain face which had been opened up by movements of the earth, then partly sealed by lava flows. He was healed, but underneath there were still one or two bruised nerves.

The death of Phyllis Henley touched these nerves into life.

One thing, however, was very clear: if the murder of Phyllis Henley was connected with the death of the

Pitts, as it surely was, then neither Terry Place nor
Edward Pitt nor Nona Pitt were guilty.

He must look for his killer elsewhere.

Oddly enough, this thought was cheering. He had
always found that once you knew where you were
wrong, then you had taken a great step towards being
right.

The picture of Christopher Court driving away from
Church Row flashed into his mind.

Never! he thought. And then: Maybe?

WHEN SERGEANT EVANS returned from Essex next
morning, he had a load of material and a headache.
He had come in early, not having been to bed, and
placed his information on Coffin's desk. Then he had
gone off to have a full breakfast in the canteen.

This might have been a mistake, he now reflected,
as he seemed to have indigestion. But it might just
have been anxiety.

'I hope I've got what the boss wants,' he said to his
friend and rival, Geoffrey Topper. 'His instructions
weren't that clear.'

'You're meant to use your intelligence,' said Topper.

'I always do that, but I'm not a mind-reader.' Topper laughed unkindly and Evans threw him a mock
bow. They were sometimes like two young puppies. 'I
mean, he can be a bit too elusive. Now you see him,
now you don't.' He looked around the room as if
Coffin might be hiding there.

'I can tell you where he is now.' Topper was an alert observer of the scene, as was wise for an ambitious young officer whose superior could be cryptic. 'Having a session with Chief Inspector Salter. Chips was sitting there waiting for him.'

'Where's Jardine?'

'Where do you think?'

'Not there.' Jardine was hardly even a joke between them any more.

'Gone to his eldest daughter's degree-giving in Birmingham.'

'And where's Lane?'

'In there with them.'

The two young men regarded each other thoughtfully.

'A row, eh?'

'Bound to be coming. And Henley getting wiped out gives Salter something to shout about. She was one of his.'

'I don't think she had much time for him. A sharp lady.'

'Where did you hear about Henley?'

'In Essex. It was all the talk. Bound to be. Ben Horridge told me himself.'

'Nice chap, is he?' Topper always liked personal details. You could never tell when they might come in useful.

'Hardly had words with him. Seemed reasonable. Non-smoker, non-drinker, that sort. He's an old pal of the boss. Did you know that?'

'Glad he's got some old friends. He sometimes seems all on his own.'

'The price of success,' said Evans sagely.

'Is that what it is?'

Raised voices came out from behind Coffin's closed door. They looked at each other pointedly. They knew more of their purpose here than they had been told, but not of all the details in the secret file in the safe in John Coffin's flat.

Evans raised an eyebrow. 'Expected Chips to be here waiting, did he?'

'Must have done. Came in with a face like thunder.' Topper was not one to strive for an imaginative simile when a well-used one came to hand.

'That must make two of them,' said Evans, as the noise of the voices came through.

'Where's Jean?' asked Evans.

'Been sent to do some shopping, I think.'

'So it's a private session? No ears wanted?'

'Looks like it.'

Again a glance of private intelligence passed between them.

They were doing a job not totally agreeable to them, but they were doing it professionally. On the other hand, there were moments that were not uncongenial.

Both of them listened to the raised voices.

Inside the room, the two men faced each other across John Coffin's desk. Paul Lane, watching, wondered if there would come a point when he would have to step between them. But no, he decided, the boss was getting colder and colder and his voice quieter. A bad sign for Salter, although he did not seem to know it.

'You stepped out of line asking Henley to do your work for you. She was off duty and should have said no.' Chief Inspector Chips Salter was an angry man. 'But of course she couldn't. So out she goes and gets herself killed.' His voice roughened. 'If it hadn't been for your interference she would still be alive.'

As this agreed with what John Coffin felt himself, he said nothing. But it did not make him more in charity with Chips Salter.

'I've said before, and I'll say it again: you are way off course about the death of the Pitts. I know this district better than you ever will, and I say it was a neighbourhood crime. I'll get the bastards who did it and it'll be one of the Costers. Probably the eldest and the youngest, they're the two worst. I've been after them for a long time and I'll get them for this.'

'And how will you get the confession, Chips?' asked Coffin in a gentle voice. 'Beat it out of them? Oh yes, I know a bit about your methods.'

Salter opened his mouth, then shut it again. His colour was ebbing.

'Hasn't it struck you that Jumbo Jardine's loose tongue operates in two ways? I know he talks to you about what goes on in this office, but I get a feedback about you.'

Salter said nothing.

'Why do you think I chose him to work with me? Because I did choose him, Chips, and quite deliberately, whatever you and he may think.'

Now the old man's moving in for the kill, thought Paul Lane, with an anticipatory flash of excitement.

'As well as your ways of getting confessions, I've learnt more than a bit about other things connected with you, Chips. Such as that holiday you took in Spain last summer and who paid. And the new car. Oh yes, and the investments you have. I should watch them if I were you, Chips, the Fraud boys from City tell me they are a bit dicey. You shouldn't have trusted the man who put you in them.'

Chips Salter stood up, his face was blotched with patches of red and white, but he was still fighting. 'Sod you! You won't get away with this. I know who to go to.'

'So do I, so do I. And the work has already been done. I was at a meeting in London yesterday where I handed over my report.'

Paul Lane looked startled. This was news even to him. Close beggar, he thought admiringly.

Coffin stood up. 'I think when you go back to your desk you will find a letter waiting for you from the Commissioner. As from today you are suspended and under investigation.'

The two young men in the outer office watched as Salter stumbled past.

'He left quietly,' said Evans.

Paul Lane walked out next. 'Got nothing to do?' he said to them as he passed.

'It's always the innocent that get blamed,' said Evans aloud.

John Coffin did not appear, his door remained closed. Sergeant Evans took an aspirin with a cup of office coffee and reflected that the Chief Superintendent was probably reading his Essex dossier now. He thought he had done a good job.

Coffin sat at his desk, surrounded by the material that Evans had collected in Essex. Photocopies, for the most part, of the originals.

On his right hand he had a pile in black and white of various comics: *Horror Gothic; The Torturer; The Monthly Guide to the Underground.*

He could only speculate what they would have been like in colour. A plentiful supply of red, he guessed. Red for blood.

These were from the room of Evelyn Bond. She had plenty of others, some English, some American, a few from Germany, and one or two from Italy and France. She might have been a linguist, but he doubted it; after all, the pictures told the story, language was not important.

Evans had also provided photographs of the boxes and contents of some games. Daniel Moore and his friends had been the source of most of these. They had had a fine collection" *Tombs and Torturers; Vices and Virgins.* And one called: *Rope and Rape.*

Evans had photographed the rules of *Tombs and Torturers.*

Players used dice and moved figures around a board. They took on roles and accepted or doled out punishments according to the rules of the game and the arbitration of The Storm Master.

In some games he was just called The Master. Or sometimes The Judge.

The penalties were nasty, violent and cruel. Throw the wrong number, and you could be, as they said, 'marked for termination', and you could choose 'between the following forms of death: poison, stabbing, shot, strangling or by a bomb'.

If carried out literally they could be murderous.

Evans had also provided a note of some cases from other countries where crimes of violence could be associated with the playing of such games.

Two youths in Texas had tried to kill the college principal, failed and poisoned themselves. Poisoning, apparently, said a handwritten note, is a common type of *T. and T.* murder. From Pennsylvania came details of a group murder, followed by the suicide of two of the killers. A girl had murdered two small children whom she was babysitting for, and had then drowned herself. In Germany there were some three deaths that the police thought could be related to such fantasy games, including one in which a self-confessed Storm Master hanged himself in prison after raping and killing his girlfriend.

There was a scribbled message attached to these last details: *Information provided by Inspector Horridge. Put together by him for his own interest.*

Coffin laid the papers aside and went to the window to look out. A bleak scene outside where it was raining hard, and he felt bleak inside. A litany of names ran through his mind, beginning with Malcolm Kincaid, the student who had killed himself, through Bill Egan, Terry Place and Irene, Edward and Nona Pitt, and ending with Phyllis Henley. It had to be the end.

Rhoda Brocklebank had a part too, although he found it hard to give it a name. A voice crying out a message which you could not always understand or believe in, but which was important. Something between the Fool as in Shakespeare and a Fury as in a Greek tragedy.

Now he thought he knew the sort of case he had to deal with, and what he had read had pointed which way to look for the killer.

He put his head round the door and spoke to Evans. 'Good work. Now here's some more.'

He gave Evans a telephone number. 'That's the personal number of a friend of mine, Captain Magrath, he's with the Philadelphia police. Talk to him, tell him all the details of what we have here and see what he says. Similar crimes, and so on.' Magrath was a police psychologist, and they had met in Rome at an international conference on violent crime. 'And don't talk about it to anyone outside the shop.'

'Wouldn't dream of it, sir,' said Evans, hurt.

As Coffin went back to his desk, he thought: It's a kind of disease. There doesn't have to be a motive.

But there he was wrong.

FOURTEEN

RHODA BROCKLEBANK was sleeping well again and eating heartily. She had talked to her friends Shirley Place and Roxie Farmer, and although they knew that they might yet face criminal charges, they had discussed it and decided they did not feel guilty. They had only done what any woman might do, and that made it all right.

She knew it was selfish to feel relief, but nevertheless, she did. She felt as though she had parcelled up her guilt and disposed of it to other people.

Her employer, John Coffin, had come in for a share, although she would have been hard put to say why he deserved it. All the same, she sensed he had got it, and was wearing it on his shoulders like a yoke.

She could almost see it when she went into his house early that morning to say she would be coming back to work and he wasn't to worry. I'm psychic, she told herself. A sensitive. I pick things up. He feels guilty.

What he had got, she couldn't have, as if there was only so much guilt going round and you had to share.

Two or three days had passed since the death of Phyllis Henley. It was hard to mark the passage of time, Coffin found. The days seemed to melt into each other and not comfortably, either. Not that he had been idle, routine had kept him busy. In this period he had received information from his friend in Philadelphia about a number of cases, involving both sexes and spanning the age range of twelve to twenty, dealing with suicides, murders and rapes connected with violent fantasy games. It made for disquieting reading. But so far he had said little about it to anyone.

Now he was sitting drinking his morning coffee when Rhoda Brocklebank arrived. It looked a poor brew, so she made him a strong cup of Indian, which anyway she fancied herself. She had to hand it to her employer, there was no nonsense about Earl Grey or Lapsang Souchong in his kitchen, but a nice straightforward Ceylon brand in leaves and not bags. She doubted if he had heard of teabags, he did not seem adventurous in his catering.

'Here you are, sir. Let me take that nasty cold mug away and give you this nice hot cup straight from the pot.'

'Thank you.' Coffin took the cup and abandoned his coffee. 'I didn't expect to see you.'

'Time I came back to work. You have to face things, don't you? But you mustn't blame yourself, sir. Not your fault, not mine. Blame the house.'

'Not sure I understand you,' said Coffin absently.

Mrs Brocklebank shrugged. 'Oh, you and I will never see eye to eye on that subject.'

He drank from the cup, rather surprised to find it was tea he was drinking, and where had she found that good china? It went back to the days of his marriage.

'Mrs Brocklebank, about the key.'

'The key?'

'The key to No. 22. You gave one to Sergeant Henley.'

'Yes. I've explained that,' said Mrs Brocklebank virtuously. 'I always had one to get in.'

'That was one key. But you must have needed another to give to Bill Egan.'

Mrs Brocklebank looked interested and slightly sly.

'I suggest you had one cut. And I guess you had more than one cut. Say two.'

Mrs Brocklebank thought about denying it, but decided not.

'So you've got one now. Will you let me have it, please?'

'I haven't got it on me.'

'So go away and get it.'

For these three days Coffin had been trying to get hold of Christopher Court, MP, but he had eluded him. Not answering his telephone and not to be found either in the London flat or in his constituency, where he had a house. He had lived in it with his wife before she had left him for a famous restaurateur. She was a woman who liked her food. She had decorated his newest eating place (she was a well-known interior decorator) and almost at once they had decided their lives matched. His agent said the MP was 'abroad', which might mean anything or nothing, but probably meant he had no idea where the Member was. The House of Commons had not seen him.

Then, this morning, as Rhoda Brocklebank departed to get the key of No. 22 for her employer, the telephone rang.

'Is that Chief Superintendent Coffin?'

'Speaking.'

'This is Christopher Court. I'm not far away. Can I come and talk?'

Coffin thought for a moment. 'Here or in my office?'

'Oh, home, please. As privately as possible. I've been wanting to talk to someone, and your sister encouraged me to try you.'

'Letty?'

'Yes. I've been with her in Scotland. Didn't you know?'

'No,' said Coffin, 'but it doesn't matter. Come right round.'

He shaved and dressed quickly, dumping the Brocklebank tea in the sink, but even so, Chris Court was there before he had slipped on his jacket.

He went down the stairs to let the man in. You shared a street door at No. 5.

'This is a kind of confessional,' said Court, as soon as they were inside Coffin's flat. 'Nice rug you've got there. Letty said you had good taste.'

'Marginal. I'm learning.' He wondered if Letty had said this, or if she believed it even if she had.

'It's too good to walk on, though. Ought to be on the wall.'

'My feet like it,' said Coffin. 'About this confessional.'

'Yes. I'm talking too much and about nothing. It's a professional habit.' He looked around. 'Do you think I could have a drink?'

'Whisky?' It was a bit early, but still . . .

'Water would do.'

'I'll make some coffee.' Once again his kettle was plugged in and the jar of coffee got out. Tea was so intractable, full of bits, leaves, so-called. He wondered if teabags would be better.

He went back into the sitting-room where Chris Court was standing by the window.

'Come on, out with it. I saw you the other day, by the way, driving down Church Row.'

'I wondered if you had. I saw you as well. Then when I heard about the murder of the policewoman I wondered if you'd suspect me of the murder.'

Coffin was silent for a moment. 'Not seriously,' he said.

'I should have spoken to you then. I'd already thought of doing so.'

'After being in Scotland with Letty?'

'Yes, I came back that day. Since then I've just been on the move, thinking.'

'I suppose it's too much to ask what you were doing with Letty? None of my business, you will say.'

'I was helping her look for your brother.' Court sounded surprised. 'I have contacts in legal circles there. My father was a Writer to the Signet.'

So it's a brother now, thought Coffin, and legal circles are involved. I hope he's not in prison.

'About the confession?' he said.

In the kitchen the kettle was beginning to boil. Both men ignored it.

'You know I was in love with Irene Pitt? I was attracted to her the first minute I saw her.'

'She was a beautiful woman.'

'Unfortunately, I was also attracted to the girl too.'

Coffin gave him a long, assessing look.

'Yes, she was very young, it was before they went to New York. Almost a child still, but that was how it was. Oh, don't worry. Nothing overt happened. But the feeling was there. And I think she knew. Irene didn't know, but Nona did.'

'Perhaps you let her know?'

Court bowed his head. 'Perhaps I did . . . I suppose you blame me.' It was a statement, not a question.

'No.' Coffin thought about his own feelings for Sarah Fleming, and measured them against what Court might have felt. Life could play you some dirty tricks, that was all he thought. He shook his head. 'No, I don't blame you.'

'I came here that day to search the house. I knew Nona kept a diary, wrote stories and anecdotes, her mother had told me. I was worried she might have talked about me. Although I had kept my distance, I had talked to her a lot: about the States—I'd been there recently—about books, pictures, games, the latest crazes. I went into the house. There was no one there, I swear that. I'm sure the policewoman was not there. I walked into the library. But then, suddenly, the feeling of the house got to me, and I couldn't stay.'

'What sort of feeling?'

Court shook his head. 'Beyond describing. I wasn't frightened, just appalled. Appalled at myself, I suppose. This was a house in which terrible things had happened and I knew I couldn't search it. I turned round and went home.'

'About what time was this?'

'Not too sure. Between ten-thirty and midnight. You might remember better yourself. You saw me.'

If he'd stayed, Coffin thought, he might have prevented the murder of Phyllis Henley just by being there.

'And you had a key?'

'Yes, I've always had a key. Irene gave me one.' Court produced it in the palm of his hand. 'Want it?'

Coffin considered. 'Yes, I'd better have it. I'll give you a note saying you have handed it to me.' He went to his desk to start writing it. Court nodded agreement.

The letter was soon written, and the writing of it had provided Coffin with a pause in which to think.

'I'll look for what the girl had written myself and see what it amounts to. I was going to take a look round the house anyway. I'll let you know what I find. If anything.'

'Thank you.'

'If it bears on the case at all, I may have to use it, otherwise . . .' He shrugged. 'We'll see. I can't promise anything.'

'Anyway, you know all there is to know now. Letty said to tell you and you'd understand. If anything does come to light about me, then I shall resign from the House. I've got no great taste for riding out a storm.'

'I'll see you out.'

On the stairs they passed Mrs Brocklebank, key in pocket, on the way in.

Coffin said, 'I don't blame you. It could happen to anyone.' He held out his hand.

Court took it.

'Thank you for saying that.'

As Coffin walked back up to his flat, he heard an indignant wail from the kitchen.

'You two gentlemen let the kettle boil dry.'

'Sorry,' said Coffin, 'it just happened.'

The usual male excuse, he thought.

HOUSES WHEN EMPTY, yet full of furniture and the equipment of day-to-day living like washing-machines and refrigerators and TV sets, show or perhaps develop a character of their own.

Coffin felt this when he stood inside the upper hall of No. 22. It was empty, but the passage of the police through it twice within weeks was clear. Dust, furniture pushed out of place, chalk marks on the floor and everywhere the powder of the fingerprint expert. The dining-room door was unsealed now, but you could still see traces of the sealing.

On his way down Church Row to make this visit, he had met Peter Fleming with a little cargo of children in tow. Weenie was there and her two brothers. Weenie called out in friendly fashion that she was dressed up for a school play.

'Hello, Weenie, hello, Peter,' he had greeted the lad. 'Where's your sister?'

Peter shrugged. 'Could be anywhere. Am I supposed to know?' He was wearing a thick sweater and had his hands thrust in his pockets. He looked cold and cross.

Weenie said in a high, penetrating but convincingly sensible voice: 'Sarah's at the Poly. It's the end of term, she has exams.' She too was wrapped up with a scarf round her throat, but in her case it seemed to be an affectation, because her dress was a flimsy organza with a frill and she had a wreath of flowers on her head. She looked like a fairy with a bad cold.

'Is that right?' Coffin looked at Peter. 'I'd like to see her.'

He meant that literally. He might not speak to her, but he certainly wanted to see her. In the flesh, living, and acting. It might resolve something for him.

'It's what she said. But I don't check up on her. Perhaps she doesn't go to the Poly as often as she claims.'

'Tell her I want to see her, will you?'

Peter shrugged. 'Can't say if she'll come. Her own law, is Sal.'

'As long as she knows.' And Coffin went into No. 22 to encounter the sense of long past living that hit him now like a wall.

He knew he had to push against this wall or it would get the better of him. It might be just imagination, probably was, but it had defeated Christopher Court and might do the same to him.

In any house over a certain age a number of people have died. But in this house the dead had faces, almost voices.

As he stood there, the procession filed past him.

Malcolm Kincaid, student.

Bill Egan, recidivist.

Terry Place, villain.

Edward, Irene and Nona Pitt, victims.

Phyllis Henley, policewoman.

There might be others behind them whose names he did not know and whose faces he could not see, but who were invisibly pushing at those in front.

He gave a shiver and opened the library door. Sunlight poured in, lighting up the books which lined the walls and gilding the furniture. Irene Pitt had created a beautiful room; the last time he had seen it had been at their party when it had been full of life and gaiety and happiness. Now a dead azalea in a pot in the window shed its last few dry blossoms in the movement of air from the door. Pale, grey and shrivelled, the petals suddenly fluttered down at his feet, the only movement in the room. Not life, just death in action, like the spasm of rigor relaxing.

On the round library table books and newspapers were laid out as if only just dropped by the reader.

No doubt the investigating police team had examined them, he told himself. Other hands came between him and dead hands.

Oh, come on, he told himself. You'd never handle a second-hand book if that was how you felt. Be your age.

His eyes fell on a book bound in pale green and lettered in gold. Out of the past, speaking on that day he had gone to the MP's flat and eaten smoked turkey sandwiches, he heard Christopher Court's voice:

'*The Book of Poisons* by Gustave Schenk. Someone had been reading it.'

Now here it was before him, on the library table.

Court could have put it there for you to find, he told himself. He doesn't have to be telling the truth when he said he found nothing. He was in the house, he admits it.

He must have left the basement door open because a current of air passed through the room, disturbing the papers and brushing more dead petals to the floor.

He closed the library door and picked up *The Book of Poisons*. It was a straightforward, well-written study of many poisons, mineral, vegetable and animal. At one time it had been well read.

A piece of paper, a torn half sheet of good quality, slipped from among the pages. *Page 83* was scribbled on it.

He turned to page 83. 'Potassium cyanide is harmless to Barn owls,' he read.

Well, now we know, he thought.

On the other side of the piece of paper was a printed letter head: *The Polytechnic of the South Side. Dept of Sociology and Contemporary History*.

Coffin did not replace the paper in the book, but laid both side by side on the table. He would collect them on his way down. He was glad he had handled them with circumspection. There would be prints.

But a pity to find what he had. He would have wished otherwise. Sarah was being dragged into this whether he liked or not.

He walked on upstairs to the bedroom floor. He had not put on weight with the years, but he was aware of a heaviness in his tread as he climbed.

Bedrooms, a bathroom, a room laid out as an office, for the benefit of Edward, he guessed. It looked unused, full of new furniture and clean-looking word processor. He must have died before he could give it substantial use. No workplace for Irene Pitt, but she had been going to leave the house and move in with Christopher Court. In any case, he did not know how she worked. She might have had an office somewhere in central London.

Here was Nona's room. Not hard to identify what was so plainly a girl's room, with rosy chintz curtains and white cane furniture. A small desk stood in the window with an alabaster lamp on it.

He moved around the room, searching. No diary. Christopher Court had been wrong there, Nona had kept no diary. Not that sort of girl. She had a few letters around, at a first glance none looked interesting.

But in a small case by the bed, he came across the folder of writings. Nona had not kept a diary, but she had written little sketches and one or two short stories.

He sat on the bed and went through them, reading quickly. Time to go back and study them more closely if he wanted.

Some of the stories and sketches were handwritten, but in a bold clear style, easy to read, while still others were neatly typed. One or two were a mixture of both, as if the writer had worked in snatches. Some of the work, presumably the earliest stuff, was childlike, on themes such as *My Friends* or *Learning to Cook,* probably school work; but the later and typewritten material was more sophisticated. That written in a mixture of both was the most personal.

I must disguise names, she had written, *because some of this will be read by outsiders. Also my mother might see it. I hope not, because she would guess who Kit and Master are. Would she know who Follower is? I guess so.*

His eye moved on. *I must never let Kit know how I feel about him. He has no idea. Or does he? Is it possible he feels the same? Just sometimes I sense he does. He does sometimes seem to offer me something not quite friendship from an adult to a child, but something a little harder. I haven't expressed that well because it is hard for me to think about it. I burn. I blush. I really do.*

This was the writing of an eager, sensuous child, just opening her mind to passion.

Well, he knew who had opened it for her.

Underneath and at the bottom of the heap, was a typed manuscript. On it, Nona had written in pencil: *Published in the School Newspaper on January 13, 1976. Third prizewinner for Best Short Story in the Junior Section.* Then she had added with an exclamation mark: *But this is not fiction!*

It was the story of two young creatures, a boy and a girl, discovering a dead body. *He was lying there under the trees with a few wet leaves on his face, which was dark and mottled. He looked as though he had drunk the poison very quickly and then fallen back dead at once. A bottle with some powder still in it was in the grass, and also a tin of Coke and a paper cup. My companion said we could leave the cup but to take the poison. It might be dangerous for any little animals that came looking for food. The little animals had already been there. They had already nibbled at the dead man's cheek.*

How much of this had really happened and how much was invention? Coffin could not tell, but some details read as truth. He decided it was all truth. Nona and one other had come across the body of a suicide, the dead man almost certainly Malcolm Kincaid.

What he also picked up was the shock and horror both young people had experienced. *He was terribly dead,* wrote Nona. *Black and swollen. And on the hands the skin was coming off. It was undignified and animal. I had never seen a dead body before, but I could not stop looking. I shall never be the same person again. I know what death is now.*

Fascinated, horrified and yet attracted, a dangerous combination.

Two young people, one of whom was Nona, the narrator, had found the body of Malcolm Kincaid. The police had already suspected the presence of someone like them. One of the pair had taken away the poison. Well, they had always known that there should have been a bottle which had contained poison on the scene of the suicide. Now he knew there had been such a bottle and he knew where it had gone.

This poison had been used to kill the Pitts.

I promised never to speak of this discovery, Nona wrote, *and I never have. But one must tell, it was too much to keep quiet. So I write this account.*

Thus keeping her word and yet clearing her soul. He had to use the word soul, it came into it somehow. Sadly, Coffin put the little story aside.

He was not at the end of his discoveries, the most significant was yet to come.

He found an advertisement cut from a black and white newspaper or comic, impossible to tell which, of a game described as the 'ultimate in fantasy games'.

He had met this game before: *Tombs and Torturers.*

Nona had written on the advertisement: *Kit sent me this. I wondered why. I think I know now and I find it exciting.*

Oh, Christopher Court, thought Coffin. You are not so innocent after all. What made you send that to Nona? But like Nona, he thought he knew too. It was a kind of invitation.

I will buy one of these for Peter, Nona had written. *Perhaps he will play with his sister. She hates me anyway. I have all she wants, and I have it without trying. She told me so herself. Just because my skin is the wrong colour.* You've got it right there, Coffin thought sadly, hating to go even so far with the theory of Chips Salter that the Pitts had been killed because of their colour.

So Nona had bought the fantasy game herself? There was a terrible irony here.

All around her was a system of loving relationships which supported her. Nona herself had fed into the system the dangerous compound of sex, aggression and fantasy which had destroyed it. She had created her own Frankenstein.

Then she had let the monster out.

A sound behind made him swing round. 'Oh, hello, Sarah. I thought you were at the Poly.' He tried to keep the shock out of his voice.

'I didn't go after all.'

'How did you get in here?'

'You left the basement door unlocked.'

'Ah.' He nodded. 'You've been here some time, haven't you? I felt a movement of air.'

'I've been sitting on the stairs, thinking what to do.'

'I should have thought that was obvious.'

'To you, not to me.' She looked at him with a half-smile. 'General confession and all that?'

'Any information you've got about these killings will be very much appreciated by me,' he said stiffly.

'I bet.' She put a hand through her hair, that bright red hair that Coffin had loved so much. Yes, he had to use that word. 'The thing is, I don't quite know what to say.'

'Oh, come on, Sarah.'

'All very well for you. You're safe inside your world. You don't know what it's like outside.' She looked at the box of papers. 'What have you got there? This is Nona's bedroom, so I suppose they are hers.'

'Nona says you hated her. Is that so?'

Sarah said: 'It certainly was true once. I was jealous, I suppose. I wouldn't say it was true now.'

'She's dead.'

'That does change things. But I assure you, hate can cross death if you want it to.'

It didn't sound like the Sarah he knew speaking. She'd picked up a false sophistication at the Poly. Or was it just nerves?

'Why did you follow me in here, Sarah?'

'You know, you know!'

He frowned. 'Oh, Sarah, you're making this hard.'

'You want me to make it easy for you? You think this isn't hard for me too?'

She sank down on the floor and covered her face with her hands.

She didn't look very dangerous like that, Coffin thought. He noticed without emotion that there were thin scratches on the back of her hands.

He advanced towards her and pulled her up. 'Come on, stand up.' The scratches on her hands were bleeding, some blood transferred itself to his own hands.

'You're bleeding.'

'Yeah.' Her voice was weary. 'Inside and out.'

There it was again, that touch of artificiality, a theatricalism that he didn't quite like in her. But after all, perhaps he shouldn't blame her. It might be the best way of dealing with the situation they found themselves in.

'How did you get those scratches?' They looked fresh.

'I had a bit of a fight.'

He felt something stiff up the arm of her sweater. He drew it out, she was unresisting. It was a knife. 'Why have you got this there?'

'It seemed the safest place to put it. You may not have noticed, but this skirt has no pocket.'

She had responded to the anger in his voice by pulling away.

'I thought you were my friend. Sergeant Henley came to our house yesterday. You must have sent her.' And indirectly, he had. 'I didn't see her but Weenie and Peter did. Weenie told me. I thought Sergeant Henley was a friend once.'

'There aren't any friends in this game.'

'I don't call it a game. And I would have thought loyalties and relationships were just what counted at a time like this.' She was dabbing at her cuts. 'You might have been more honest with me, come to me, told me what you were thinking.'

But he hadn't known what he was thinking until so very recently. Or not been willing to put it into words.

'Well, anyway, I didn't suspect you of murder.'

'Thanks for nothing.' She was preoccupied with her cuts.

'Where did you get the knife?'

'It's one of my kitchen knives. Was. I don't suppose I'll be using it again.' The knife had been sharpened to a wicked point.

She added: 'I've missed two other knives.'

'How did you get the scratches?'

'Looking for it. I found it hidden in a climbing rose in the garden, the rose fought back. You could hide a body in that tangle. I knew it was there somewhere, Weenie told me she saw him put it there. Weenie sees everything.'

'And you were bringing it to me?'

'I was bringing it here. I was thinking of dumping it on the scene of the crime... Then I found out you were here.'

He didn't think that was quite true, he thought she had known and had meant to bring him the knife, but did not now like to say so. Family loyalty was a strange business.

So this was the knife that had killed Phyllis Henley. She must have identified the murderer and come here looking for proof. After all, she had known the Fleming family well. What had the woman come to this house looking for? What he had found himself, probably, the written evidence from Nona. Somehow she had guessed of its existence.

'Come on, Sarah, let's get you out of here.' He wrapped the knife in his handkerchief. There would probably be no fingerprints but you had to try. Almost certainly be blood traces, though.

They walked down the stairs together.

'Did you get mixed up with these fantasy games?'

Sarah shook her head. 'Knew about it. Tried a postal game once. But it wasn't my scene. I thought it was a joke.'

'No joke.'

'I know that now. I had two games. That was enough. The Master, self-appointed as far as I could see (I found out afterwards he was someone I knew at the Poly), told me I was deemed his whipping-boy. I wasn't having any of that.'

Coffin thought of the games being played here and elsewhere. It was only just beginning now. Where would the infection be in ten years' time?

'Nona played this game? With Terry Place and Peter?'

'They gave her a role.'

'Did Nona let Peter have a key to this house?'

Sarah nodded. 'I think so. I know he had one.'

'What about Terry Place. How did he get into this?'

'We've always known him. He's local. He and Peter had a lot in common. They liked old things, talking about history, feeling they were both great and in charge, like you could with the game. And of course, Terry did hate Mr Egan. He won the right to execute him. So Peter said.'

The scrap of paper with Egan's address on it had probably come from Peter through the no doubt unconscious channel of Mrs Rhoda Brocklebank, thought Coffin. Wherever you turned, she was.

'And that was the point of the meeting in the tunnel? It was a play in the game?' And the tunnel was the Tomb. He could understand the fascination now.

'Yes, but I don't think Peter thought Place would go as far as he did. Peter loved Nona, he really did, he saved her life then, remember.'

'Why did he kill her afterwards, then? Because he did poison Edward, Irene and Nona Pitt, didn't he? He had the poison and he used it.'

'Love can turn very sour sometimes,' said Sarah. 'They dismissed him, you see, the Pitts did. After he had saved Nona, they paid him off.'

'How?'

'They thanked him and gave him money. They said it was for his education. The terrible thing is, I think they meant it well. But it showed they just never thought of Peter as a match for their Nona. And Nona went along with it. It was cruel.'

'I see.'

'They blamed Peter, but it wasn't really his fault, it just happened.'

Did such a terrible sequence of events just happen? Privately, he thought there had been a bond of violence between Nona and Peter ever since they stumbled across the body of Malcolm Kincaid. That had been the real beginning for those two, the rest had followed from it.

And yet Sarah had seen her parents die tragically, comically, without turning towards evil. Sarah was good.

She was crying now, tears rolling down her cheeks.

'Come on.' He took Sarah into the kitchen, gave her a glass of water, and took one himself.

At the basement door they met Peter Fleming. He had a knife in each hand, held in clenched fists, each pointed blade directed towards them. On his hands and forearms were the gouged out and bloody scratches that Phyllis Henley, fighting for her life, had given him.

'You stinker, Sal.'

'I went a long way with you, Peter. But no more.'

Peter slammed the door behind him, and leaned against it. There was a flashy brightness in his eyes. His menace seemed directed at his sister, he was ignoring Coffin.

'Crying for Nona, Sarah?'

She did not answer. Coffin tried to put his body between her and her brother, but she edged aside.

'You ought to be crying for me. I loved her, I saved her life, and they paid me off. I wasn't good enough. They were black, and rich, and I wasn't good enough for their daughter.'

Black, thought Coffin, like my dearest Letty, who is palest coffee cream and lovely. At that moment he hated Peter with a vivid personal dislike. 'She had to be punished. It was my right.' He raised his head, and for the first time looked Coffin in the eyes. 'I make the rules, policeman. I am the Master.'

Sarah saw what he was about to do before Coffin and flung herself forward. Peter knocked her backwards, then turned one knife inwards and dug it deep inside himself.

While still erect, he plunged the other knife straight into Coffin's side.

Coffin could hear Sarah screaming, saw Peter sink to the ground, and as his own blood spurted out and the sense of weakness began at once, he found himself thinking:

Am I going to live to see whom Letty has flushed out in Scotland?

Then the sentence shrank and seemed to march in capital letters across his consciousness.

WILL I LIVE?

He made a tremendous effort of will to hang on to consciousness. I won't die, he thought defiantly. I refuse.

But in this house, who could be sure?

THE UNDERGROUND STREAM

VELDA JOHNSTON

AN OLD HOUSE WITH...EVEN OLDER SECRETS

For twenty-four years, Gail Loring has fought both her fear of the alcoholic haze in which the women of her family have lived *and* the haunting images of a man—her great-great-great-grandfather—called the Monster of Monroe Street.

Now Gail can run no longer. At her ancestral home in the summer resort town of Hampton Harbor, she vows to confront the past. She finds herself stepping back into the stream of time. She is Martha Fitzwilliam, a young wife and mother who lived here more than a hundred and fifty years ago. Gail shares Martha's secrets...and feels her terror. A terror she must pursue to its ultimate act of shattering violence....

"The vicissitudes of time and place are skillfully evoked in this eerie and often dream-like novel." —*Publishers Weekly*

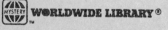

OTHER PEOPLE'S HOUSES

SUSAN ROGERS COOPER

In Prophesy County, Oklahoma, the unlikely event of a homicide is coupled with the likely event that if one occurs, the victim is somebody everybody knows....

And everybody knows nice bank teller Lois Bell who, along with her husband and three kids, dies of accidental carbon monoxide poisoning. But things just aren't sitting right with chief deputy Milton Kovak. Why were the victims' backgrounds completely untraceable? And why was the federal government butting its nose in the case?

"Milt Kovak tells his story with a voice that's as comforting as a rocking chair and as salty as a fisherman."

—*Houston Chronicle*

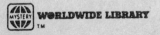

First Time in Paperback

ELIZABETH TRAVIS

LOSERS WEEPERS

Hoping to acquire publishing rights to the final manuscript of recently deceased literary giant Charles Melton, Ben and Carrie Porter take a working vacation to his Riviera home. They're shocked to find the masterpiece in sections, each one bequeathed to a different heir. Whoever can collect the complete book will own the copyright—and be guaranteed a financially secure future.

Was Charles Melton an evil-minded scamp who set up this devilish scheme in the spirit of revenge? Or did he simply want all his heirs to reveal their true natures? When two of Melton's heirs are murdered, the Porters begin to suspect that a clever author had stuffed his final masterpiece with secrets—deadly secrets—which a killer intends to keep hidden at all costs.

Ben and Carrie are "two likeable, 30-something amateur sleuths."

— Publishers Weekly

B. M. GILL

the Fifth Rapunzel

First Time in Paperback

AN INSPECTOR MAYBRIDGE MYSTERY

THE SUDDEN DEATH OF PROFESSOR PETER BRADSHAW AND HIS WIFE WAS RULED ACCIDENTAL....

But in light of the forensic pathologist's damning testimony in the Rapunzel murder cases—in which five prostitutes were strangled, long hair wrapped around their necks in a noose—Detective Chief Inspector Tom Maybridge decided to gently remind Bradshaw's teenage son that his father *did* have enemies....

Nobody had paid attention to the convicted killer's fervent tirades condemning Bradshaw's false testimony on the "Fifth Rapunzel." Perhaps it was time to listen.

"A cunningly twisted suspense mystery."
—*New York Times Book Review*

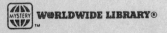

A GINNY TRASK AND FRANK CARVER MYSTERY

First Time In Paperback

COLD TRACKS

LEE WALLINGFORD

BLOOD LEAVES A DEADLY TRAIL

Tired of the violence of big-city crime, former narcotics agent Frank Carver trades the streets of Seattle for the penny-ante stuff of Oregon's Neskanie National Forest. Work is wonderfully, refreshingly dull for the forest's new law-enforcement officer. No shootings. No bodies. No murders.

Until the corpse of Nino Alvarez, an immigrant worker, is found in the woods by fire dispatcher Ginny Trask.

Skillful debut. This intriguing pair of detectives—a burned-out cop and a beautiful young widow—promise future entertaining reading."

—*Publishers Weekly*

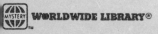

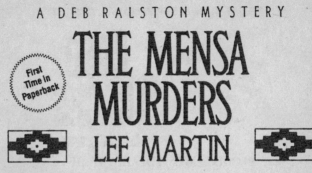

A DEB RALSTON MYSTERY

THE MENSA MURDERS

First Time in Paperback

LEE MARTIN

DEAD BODIES LEAVE NO TRAILS....

Three women are murdered—in identical and very unusual ways. The killer is solicitous—first breaking their necks, then tucking them neatly into bed before cleaning the house and tending to the pets.

With no trail to follow—since the killer insists on straightening up the mess—Fort Worth detective Deb Ralston looks beyond the scrubbed floors to discover the victims were all members of Mensa, an organization for the superintelligent. Deb quickly discovers that the group's members are not all as sane as they are smart.

"A believable sleuth in a superior series." —*Booklist*

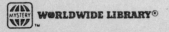